'At the first scent of burning heather on the breeze, Oak had scrambled to the highest branch of the fir. He could see the billowing smoke-clouds, lit from underneath by the red and orange flames, coming downwind towards them on an ever widening front. Coming too fast to race away from, particularly with Old Burdock unable to move quickly. There was a chance that if they stayed in the tree the flames might not reach them, but he had once seen a burning tree and was not going to risk that. There was only one other option . . .'

Michael Tod was born in 1937 in Dorset, where this story is set. He lived near Weymouth until his family moved to a hill farm in Wales when he was eleven. His childhood experiences on the Dorset coast and in the Welsh mountains have given him a deep love and knowledge of wild creatures and the countryside, which is reflected in his poetry and in this, his first novel. Married, with three children and three grandchildren, he still lives, works and walks in his beloved Welsh hills, but visits his old haunts in Dorset whenever he can. Michael Tod is currently working on the third volume of the saga, *The Final Flight*.

BY THE SAME AUTHOR

The Second Wave

THE SILVER TIDE

Michael Tod

ORION

An Orion paperback
First published in Great Britain by Cadno Books in 1993
This edition first published by Orion in 1994
This paperback edition published in 1994 by Orion Books Ltd,
Orion House, 5 Upper St Martin's Lane, London WC2H 9EA

A CIP catalogue record for this book is available from the
British Library.

ISBN: 1 85797 319 4

Printed in England by Clays Ltd, St Ives plc

To the Dispossessed

This is a work of fiction. Names, characters and
incidents are either the product of the author's imagination
or used fictitiously. Any resemblance to actual events or
squirrels living or dead is entirely coincidental.

Maps

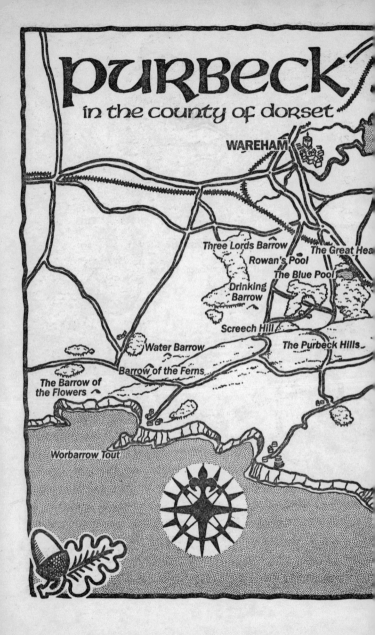

purbeck
in the county of dorset

WAREHAM

Three Lords Barrow

The Great Hea

Rowan's Pool

The Blue Pool

Drinking
Barrow

Screech Hill

Water Barrow

The Purbeck Hills

Barrow of the Ferns

The Barrow of
the Flowers ⌃

Worbarrow Tout

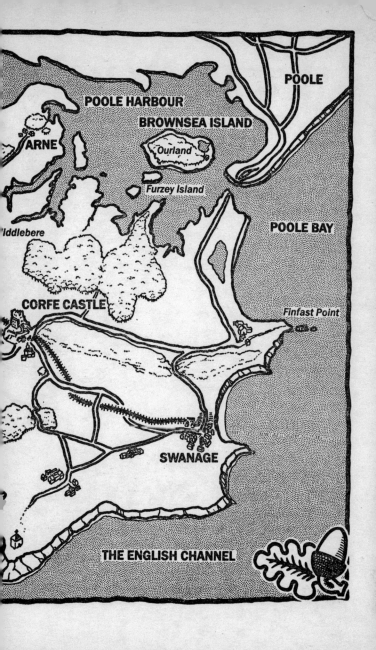

Chapter 1

The year was nineteen sixty-one. Humans symbolised this as 1 9 6 1 but, as all humans know, such symbols are meaningless to lesser creatures.

Marble sat on top of the World. Actually it was a fence-post with slack strands of rusting wire joining his post to those on either side of him, on one of which his companion and acolyte, Gabbro, was sitting, tearing the limbs off a fledgling with his sharp yellow teeth.

The World around them was Dorset, in the south of England, or New America as his kind liked to call it.

A male grey squirrel in the prime of life, Marble licked the blood from his lips and looked out across the Great Heath to the hills of Purbeck beyond. Out there was Adventure, Advancement and Achievement!

He flicked his tail at the blackbirds, the parents of the babies he and Gabbro had just taken from their nest in a hawthorn bush and killed, annoyed at the way they flew at his head in protest, shouting "Chit, chit, chit. Chit, chit, chit."

"Chit to you too," he shouted back and Gabbro, sworn to silence for the journey, grinned over at him.

Marble had invented the "Vow of Silence" on the second day out as noisy, inquisitive youngsters learned more if they kept their mouths shut and their ears and eyes open.

"Tomorrow we probe Purbeck," Marble called across, proud to be an Explorer, Missionary and Disturber of the Peace.

There had been patches of snow on the ground under the trees when Marble and Gabbro had left Home-Base at Woburn Park, moons before. Having received his instructions from the Great Lord Silver, he had wasted no time in leaving; better to be out adventuring than hanging about in idleness with the plotters and the hangers-on.

He had chosen a promising youngster with the name of Gabbro to be his acolyte and, when they had set out together, he had only glanced back once at the cluster of dreys forming the New America Base. These dreys were almost completely hidden amongst the branches, each round, woven mass of twigs and leaves the retreat of one of the senior governing families. Each so high and well concealed that human Visitors passing underneath seldom noticed them.

Ever since the first grey squirrels from America had been released there, in what the humans called the eighteen nineties, Woburn had been the centre of their operations.

The toughest, meanest Grey in that first batch had taken charge and called himself Lord Silver. It had seemed to him that grey was a drab sort of colour and it *was* true that in certain conditions, the light-coloured guard-hairs projecting through the squirrels' fur made them look silvery. Anyway, he was chief and could call himself by any name he wished.

Lord Silver had soon become Great Lord Silver and there had been a Great Lord Silver at Woburn ever since. When one died, others fought for his rank and position. The winner, if he survived his wounds, would then impose his ideas and prejudices on the others.

Marble had been glad to be away. He hated the intrigue and the plotting of the Oval Drey, and the current occupant was far too permissive in many ways for Marble's taste. Maybe, when he, Marble, had made a real name for himself he might . . . No – get on with the job in hand! Purbeck was a real challenge. Somewhere where he could prove himself.

His training had finished with his return from that trip to the west, keeping north of the Great River and penetrating as far as the Ford of the Oxen, though the name of the place, once given to it by the native red squirrels, seemed inappropriate.

It was an honour now to have been given the chance to explore and soften up this place the natives called Purbeck. Very little was known of it and he and Gabbro would be the first Silvers to probe there.

On that first day out he had hopped along, Gabbro chattering excitedly at his side.

"No – I don't know why it's called Purbeck! Yes – it is a long way. No – I haven't been there before." An acolyte was all very well, they could be useful at times, and every ambitious youngster had to learn, but . . .

Marble had scented an acorn under the leaf litter, probably buried by a fellow squirrel, or perhaps a jay, the previous autumn. He had dug it up and eaten it rapidly while Gabbro had searched around until he too had found one. Marble then moved on, Gabbro following, awkwardly holding the acorn in his teeth, snatching a bite whenever Marble stopped to choose a route. Gabbro clearly had a mass of questions he wanted to ask but, with an acorn in his mouth, he had been forced to keep them until later.

Spring had come and passed as the pair made steady progress towards the west and south. They had passed through Silver country all the way, meeting no native red squirrels. Marble had thought how satisfying it was to see the success his kind had at exploiting the countryside, and with the population pressure behind him building up inexorably, more land *was* needed. What was that term that the Great Lord Silver had used? "Leaping-room!" That had summed it up precisely.

He, Marble, had been chosen personally for this mission. He might not agree with all that Woburn stood for now, but if the chief had sent him, it was up to him as a loyal Silver to do his very best.

There were Reds still holding out in parts of southern New America and there were reputed to be Reds still skulking in this place they called Purbeck, who might never have heard of the Silver Tide sweeping irresistibly their way. They were not dangerous, more of a nuisance really, but they did cling on so to what they called their Guardianships. Such primitive ideas! How could they be so naïve? And the Sun business that he had heard tell of—well!

They had lingered a little in what the colonists called the New Forest, though it was obviously very old. Had he not had a mission, Marble might have been tempted to stay on and fight for a territory there. Even he had been moved by the beauty of the place when the sunlight, striking through

4

the new green leaves of the gnarled oak trees, had lit up the forest floor and shone on the dappled coats of the fallow deer that passed below.

It was here that he had shown Gabbro the Stone force.

Each night, before finding a suitable sleeping place, Marble had instructed his now silent acolyte to collect stones and lay them out in the square patterns, and how to activate the force by his body power.

Marble enjoyed watching the concentration and concern showing on Gabbro's face as he made squares with four stones on each side and then when Marble told him to, reached out apprehensively to place his paw on one of the corner stones. The invisible Earth force could be whisker-sensed as it was drawn from the ground and diverted upwards to treetop height in the shape of a toadstool. Any creature getting too near was paralysed, although, as Marble himself had learned in his training, a certain degree of immunity could be acquired.

Gabbro had quickly become adept at laying out the Power Squares and bracing himself for the drain on his body energy as he started the force going. Marble knew that the energy to start a four by four square would be restored by a night's sleep but, even so, he preferred Gabbro to be the one to supply it. He had expended enough of his own energy during *his* training.

Between the New Forest and Purbeck they overtook colonising groups also pressing south and west, each group dealing with the few remaining Reds in whatever way they chose, harassing them until they moved on, leaving the best woods to be taken over and settled by the Greys.

Now Marble and Gabbro had come to the edge of the

heathland which was as far as the earlier explorers had penetrated. They had not reported how hot it would be here, but maybe this heat was exceptional. New America was noted for the vagaries of its weather!

Somewhere across the heather, beyond the birches and the pines, was Purbeck – his challenge!

Gabbro had finished eating the fledgling, so Marble flicked the "follow me" signal with his tail and leapt to the ground.

The youngster followed, and the blackbirds, still scolding, flew to the fence-posts and perched there, calling after the two strange creatures as they hopped away along the dusty path through the heather stems.

Marble ignored their calls. He knew that the birds could not harm him and there were other real dangers to watch for. But most of all, he was alert for signs of native Reds. Their presence would mean good squirrel country – country suitable for colonisation!

Rowan the Bold was lost. Not the heart-thumping, stomach-twisting feeling of being lost that hits a dreyling when it first looks around on the ground and cannot see its parents, but the "Where, in the name of the Sun, am I now?" sort of being lost.

It was bad enough to be on the ground amongst all this heather, where he felt vulnerable, but he must get his bearings or he could wander around lost for hours and that would be a poor way to finish his climbabout.

Standing up to his full red squirrel height, he could just see over the tops of the heath plants and he looked for a tree, as a shipwrecked sailor on a raft searches for an island and the security that this implies. The only tree that he could see was a stunted birch about the height of a Man, growing out of a bank of whitish-grey clay further along the path. The peaty dust from the parched soil tickled his throat as he hopped towards it, glancing over his shoulder from time to time to make sure that no hungry fox or playful dog was following. "Come on," he said to himself, "don't be a squimp, remember your tag. You're Rowan the Bold."

He scrambled up the bank and climbed the tree, feeling the comfort of being off the ground and the joy of his claws biting into the smooth bark. He climbed until the tree started to sag sideways with his weight, then paused to enjoy a tiny breeze which ruffled his fur and fluffed out the hairs of his tail.

Now, where am I? he wondered, peering around as he clung to the swaying stem. Through the heat-haze he could see a line of pine trees but not in any familiar pattern, and turning his head he could see the ridge of the Purbeck Hills. Studying their outline, he knew that he had come too far west. He was about to drop to the ground and head off eastwards towards home, when he caught the faintest whiff of water-scent on the air.

Rowan turned his head slowly, testing the scent and trying for a direction. It seemed to be floating to him from just beyond the pine trees. His mouth was dry and the idea of a cool drink drove thoughts of home into second place. Dropping on to the clay bank, he headed towards the pines.

The line of trees formed, vanished and re-formed in the haze ahead as he followed a twisting path through the heather, bracken and furze in the shimmering desert of the Great Heath.

Reaching the trees, he was tempted to rush down to the water and slake his thirst, but instinct and training had taught him to proceed more cautiously.

In a strange country,
Be careful. Time spent looking
Is seldom wasted.

He climbed the nearest tree and ran out along a branch to look down on to the pool below. It was not quite as big as the one at home, the Blue Pool, and certainly not as dramatically coloured. This one was a delicate orangey brown, but the water was clear enough from above for him to see the white of the clay bottom, well below the surface. It was surrounded by a low sand-cliff and in one place, where the clay must have been of too poor a quality for the long-dead quarrymen to have bothered with it, an over-grown mound remained, surrounded on all sides by water, and topped by three well-grown trees. Across the pool where the cliff had collapsed in places, the quartz particles in the sand caught the rays of the sun, now quite low in the sky, making them sparkle and gleam.

Air smelling of warm damp moss rose from the water's edge to mingle deliciously with the resin-scent of bark on the hot pine trunks. Huge pink and white flowers set amongst dark green circular leaves fringed the pool, leaving a large clear area in the centre.

Rowan watched a green dragonfly alight on a lily pad to rest for a moment, curl its tail under the leaf and lay an egg before rising and circling away. There were many damsel-flies flitting over the water, smaller than the dragons, some flying in mating pairs.

From high above, the pool was the shape of a hunched animal, perhaps a rabbit with his ears down, thought Rowan, the hump of land above the water being just where its eye would be. There was no scent nor sense of danger but he went slowly down the trunk head-first, looking about him as he did so.

> *A watchful squirrel*
> *Survives to breed and father –*
> *More watchful squirrels.*

He drank at the water's edge, glanced at the sun to measure its angle and decided to stay there for the night. He could be home in one or two days at the most. There was plenty of food about, no sign of other squirrels having foraged there, and he ate until comfortably full, then chose a tree to sleep in. It was too warm to think of making even the most rudimentary drey for shelter, so he made himself at home in a fork of one of the tallest of the pines and fell asleep; to dream of the beautiful pool below him, with its sparkling sand, water-flowers, dragonflies and the "Eyeland" at the far end.

Chapter 2

Old Burdock, the Tagger Squirrel, sitting in a tree above a lake of sapphire blue water, watched the dreylings at play, the bright early morning sunlight glowing on their ruddy brown fur. Soon it would be her job to give them a tag which would stay with them for their lifetime. Unless, that is, they earned another, better tag through some outstanding act or impressive behaviour. Then a special Council Meeting would consider her recommendation for a change.

Ambitious squirrels were always hoping and working for an up-tag. This was good for the community. Not so pleasant was when she had to propose a down-tag for unsquirrel-like behaviour or worse.

She must always remember the code by which she worked, taught in the pattern of words used for all the symbolic and cultural traditions of her race.

> *Tagging a squirrel*
> *As reward or punishment*
> *Is a weighty task.*

This arrangement of sounds, five, then seven, then five

again, had a special authority and all squirrel lore was embodied in Kernels like this.

Only recently the Council had had to downgrade Juniper and Bluebell, the Guardians of Humanside, for scrounging food from the Visitors who came to the Blue Pool and who ate at the stone Man-dreys in that Guardianship. Since then Juniper and Bluebell, now tagged the Scavengers, had kept to their own side of the pool, lowering their tails in shame when they saw other squirrels, but there was no evidence yet of them mending their ways. Burdock knew how powerful the effect of a bad tag could be. A squirrel carrying the burden of a denigratory tag would have low self-esteem and be unable to mate, thus ensuring that only squirrels conforming to acceptable standards of squirrel behaviour would produce and raise youngsters. It was Old Burdock's burdensome task, as Tagger, to keep an eye on the behaviour of the whole community, and to allocate "True Tags" without favouritism.

On the winding Man-paths below her, human Visitors would soon be strolling, admiring the views glimpsed between the trees, most not giving any thought to the possibility of their being watched by squirrels from above.

These Visitors would come all through the summer, arriving in cars and coaches to park in the field which was a part of the Humanside Guardianship. They would wander under the pines, their cameras clicking in an attempt to capture the beauty and the "blueness" of the famous pool.

The size of a small field, this pool, like Rowan's, had once been a clay quarry, providing high quality blue ball-clay to make tobacco pipes and Wedgwood pottery and for use in refining sugar as it was made into sugarloaves, those cone-shaped blocks after which so many mountains have been named all across the world. Now, nearly a century after the workings had been abandoned, some unique combination of suspended clay particles and concentrated minerals in the rainwater trapped there gave it the name by which it was known. The Blue Pool was now on the itinerary of all Visitors to Purbeck.

Burdock looked out over the water, then resumed her watch on the dreylings. One, her own granddaughter, was outstanding – Marguerite, the only dreyling this year of Oak the Cautious and Burdock's daughter, Fern the Fussy, who were the current Guardians of Steepbank on the opposite side of the pool to Humanside. Oak combined this role of Guardianship with that of Council Leader and was inordinately fond of Marguerite.

Intelligent, active and charismatic, definitely a youngster to watch. Could be Council Leader herself one day, thought Burdock. Not common to have a female for leader but there is no taboo. If not Leader, then she may take over my job when I am Sun-gone. A mixed batch the rest, though.

Soon it would be time for Rowan the Bold, Marguerite's brother from the previous year, to be home from his climbabout. She was looking forward to hearing about his exploits. Sharing the active experiences of the youngsters seemed a fair repayment for the time she had spent in passing on the lessons her years had taught her.

Some of them, knowing that she was watching, showed off, leaping from branch to branch and demonstrating their developing prowess in any way they thought would impress.

Earning a good tag
Is each squirrel's ambition –
Then to retain it.

She envied them their youthful energy and remembered with a sigh just how it felt to test oneself by leaping greater and greater distances and the excitement and relief of landing safely in the branches beyond. Now, even a small jump across a modest gap tired her and she often found it easier to go down one tree trunk and up another. She felt she was too old to risk a fall.

Burdock cocked her head, listening. Across the pool came the sound of the metal gates at Humanside being unlocked, the signal for the squirrels to retreat into the upper branches and lie out on the resinous bark, enjoying the sunshine and any light breezes filtering through the treetops. They were safe there from foxes and the dogs of human Visitors, and no hawks big enough to be dangerous had been seen for many years. The once dreaded pine marten was now only an ancestral memory and a bogey to frighten unruly youngsters with marten-dread. Burdock recalled the old Kernel:

Pine marten's sharp teeth
Bite off the ears and the tails
Of naughty dreylings.

She moved to the highest branch of the tallest tree on Steepbank above where the sand-cliff dropped almost sheer to the water's edge. Not only was there the best chance of catching any breezes, but from there she had the finest

14

view, and it was her job to watch and report on any unusual happenings. She looked across towards Humanside and the Man-dreys. The Red-Haired Girl was there. No danger from her – never has been – almost one of us, she thought.

Nothing was moving at Deepend to her right paw side: the guardians there would already be resting and no Visitors had arrived so far. She looked at Beachend to her left, all quiet there too, the sandy beach gleaming in the sun, curving round beyond the blue of the water. Sun, how she loved this place! Burdock stretched out and closed her eyes, reflecting on the part she had taken in building this happy community.

There was now a clear recognition of the place the Sun played in all their lives. She had gradually got rid of that old concept of worship. Respect was a much better term. The Sun could surely not want worshipping, it was far too all-wise for that.

The selection of Leaders and the establishment of the Council for the Demesne had largely been her idea. After a disastrous run of First-borns taking automatic control, regardless of their abilities, she had at last been able to get the demoralised squirrels to give her ideas a try. The worst that any squirrel could complain of now was boredom.

Old Burdock drifted off to sleep as the first pair of humans strolled along the path round the deep end of the pool, the male fanning his face with his summer straw hat.

At two o'clock, the Red-Haired Girl who was the waitress at the Tea Rooms was clearing the tables, the lunchtime rush over.

That pair of squirrels was hanging around again waiting

for any scraps to be thrown to them. She had noticed that one seemed particularly fond of salted peanuts and she idly wondered what it thought of the unusual taste, and was about to fetch a packet from the display of snacks when a visitor called to her, asking for another cup of coffee.

The squirrels were forgotten.

Chapter 3

Precisely at five o'clock, Tom, the caretaker, swung the big metal gates shut, collected his litter-bag and walked away to pick up the cigarette packets and ice-cream wrappers that somehow had not found their way into the waste-bins.

Burdock stretched one leg after another and looked down on to the network of paths. The Visitors had all gone, the Human Who Picked Things Up, now down at Beachend, was a part of the landscape and quite harmless, so it was safe to come down and forage for pine cones and early fungi. Halfway down the tree she stopped and stared.

Two creatures were coming along the path. They moved like squirrels but were much bigger than any squirrel she had ever seen — and grey!

Burdock watched from the tree trunk as the unfamiliar animals advanced. They progressed in a series of short dashes, pausing between each to look round. The leading one saw Burdock, stopped and sat up.

"What place is this?"

"You are in the Guardianship of Oak the Cautious, in the Blue Pool Demesne. I am Burdock, the Tagger."

"Greetings, Burdock," said the Grey. "I am called

Marble. This is my companion, Gabbro. We bring salutations from the Great Lord Silver, to whom we all owe allegiance." He held his right paw diagonally across his chest.

"Are you squirrels?" asked Burdock.

"We are. Squirrels of the Silver Kind. Our ancestors came from the Great Lands far away over the water beyond the sunset, but we are now bringing enlightenment to this land." He raised his tail proudly.

Burdock considered his action unmannerly. It was not proper to raise your tail until you had been greeted by the local guardian.

> Stranger, show respect
> You are the alien here.
> Teach us to trust you.

"What is your business?" asked Burdock, her voice sharp.

"Are you the Senior Squirrel in this precinct?" asked Marble coldly.

The word was new to Burdock but she understood its meaning. "No, I'm the Tagger, Oak the Cautious is the Council Leader."

"Take us to his drey," commanded Marble.

"As you wish," said Burdock and, holding her tail as high as possible, she set off in the direction of Oak's drey in the Council Tree.

Other squirrels had watched the confrontation and followed Burdock, Gabbro and Marble along the path. Burdock suddenly climbed a tree to see if the strangers could climb. They could. She forced herself to race along a branch as fast as she could and then leap to another tree. The Greys followed effortlessly. They *were* squirrels!

By the time they reached Oak's drey there were half a dozen more squirrels following them. Oak heard the movements in the branches before he could see the cause and moved higher for a better view. He was as surprised as Old Burdock had been to see the grey creatures which now approached, their tails low. "Greetings, strangers," said Oak, looking at Burdock for an explanation.

"Greetings, Oak the Cautious," said Burdock. "These strangers of the Silver Kind have come with 'salutations' from *their* Leader." She paused uncomfortably, still resenting the ill manners of the Greys and the high-handed way Marble had spoken to her. Taggers were second only to Council Leaders and should be treated with respect.

Oak looked with interest at the two Greys. They were larger than any of the Reds, more heavily built, and their ears were round without any trace of tufts on them. Their eyes were different too, seeming not to look straight at him. He did not feel he could trust them.

"So, you can speak our tongue," said Oak.

"After a fashion, Cautious Oak," said Marble. "We bring salutations from the Great Lord Silver and, as you are the local chief, seek your permission to teach the power of numbers to your subjects."

"I have no subjects, Marble the Stranger, these are all Respecters of the Sun, Guardians of the Land. I am just their chosen Leader. What are these numbers of which you speak?"

"In due course, in due course," replied Marble

dismissively, looking round to see if the other squirrels were listening. They were. "First I wish to learn of your local customs and then to rest from my journey." He held his tail low in a gesture of deference, during which display no reasonable request can be refused.

> *A submissive stance*
> *And a request, presumes help –*
> *Give it if you can.*

"What do you wish to know, Marble the Stranger?" asked Oak.

"I suppose you consider the Sun to be the provider of everything, like the other natives who inhabited the middle lands?" said Marble.

Oak nodded assent. Could there be any doubt about that? This he had been taught by his Tagger when he was a dreyling and the evidence was to be seen everywhere. Plants started to grow when warmed by the Sun. The squirrel dreylings were born after the warmth of the spring Sun had aroused their parents to courtship. It was obviously the Sun that ripened the nuts and pine cones in the autumn to provide their winter food stocks.

> *The life-giving Sun*
> *Provides all we need. Father*
> *Of all the squirrels.*

"Yes," said Oak positively, "that is our belief."

His mate, Fern the Fussy, was only half listening. An obstinate blob of resin was sticking to the hairs of her tail.

She combed it with her claws, then tried to lick off the residue. In the end she had to bite away a few hairs. She combed again to cover the gap. After all she was the Council Leader's life-mate and would be expected to look her best, especially when there were important visitors. She nipped off a twig which was sticking out of a branch at an untidy angle.

"What number comes after eight?" asked Marble.

"There is no number after eight," replied Oak. "We only have eight front claws to count on. After that there are 'lots'. "

"Great Lord Silver," Marble said quietly, glancing at the silent Gabbro and fighting to keep his tail from rising with superiority. "It seems you still practise guardianship instead of possession?"

"This word – possession – is unknown to me," said Oak.

"Possession, ownership, what's mine is mine, what's yours is yours, for as long as you can keep it. The only civilised way to behave, everybody knows where they are. Surely you can understand that?"

Oak tried, but the concept was beyond him. It was like trying to think about how far the land stretched away from the Blue Pool. Beyond it was the heath, or fields or woods, and beyond them, more. What was beyond those? They must stop somewhere, but where? He had heard about the Sea but had never seen it. What was beyond the Sea? He had often puzzled over this enigma but had had to give up, unsatisfied, and other duties had prevented him ever having gone climbabout as some of the more adventurous squirrels did when they were young.

This concept of ownership was the same. A squirrel

couldn't "own" a tree or a path or a glade! The idea didn't make sense. *Guardianship* was clear. From the treetops, squirrels could watch out for anything that might be harmful or unnatural. Not that they could always do anything about it, he thought ruefully. At least some of the humans must feel the same. One of them, the Human Who Picked Things Up, did keep the whole of the demesne free of other humans' litter.

"Any special customs or rituals?" asked Marble.

By now virtually all the squirrels of the community were listening. News of the strangers' arrival had quickly spread through the demesne.

"Nothing that comes to mind," said Oak after a pause, "unless you mean the Sun-tithe, where we dig up and eat only seven out of every eight nuts we hide. We've always done that."

> *One out of eight nuts*
> *Must be left to germinate.*
> *Here grows our future.*

Marble was disappointed; he had learned about native behaviour from his mentor the previous year, and there appeared to be nothing dramatically different here. No natives ever understood the importance of ownership. "Just another lot of thick Reds," he would have to report to Woburn. It was all so boring. They all seemed obsessed by this Sun idea, as if the sun would care about any of them! Take and hold was the only way. The sun's there, always has been, always will be, and that's that, he thought superciliously. But the area is good, plenty of food and the surroundings are attractive.

22

If the Great Lord Silver was pleased with him he might put in a claim for this precinct for himself when he reported back.

"We will rest now," he said. "Tomorrow I'll teach you something about the power of numbers, and indeed Stone force. With your permission," he added, looking at Oak and keeping his tail lowered with difficulty. These natives were so naïve!

Oak looked round, saw his daughter, Marguerite, and said, "Please escort our guests to the Strangers' Drey, Daughter, and see that they have food."

The dreyling skipped about. "I am Marguerite the Bright One. Please follow me, Marble the Stranger, Gabbro the Companion."

She led them to the drey kept for squirrels passing through and checked that the supply of nuts and other delicacies was adequate.

"Is there anything else you would like?" she asked innocently.

Marble looked her over. Only a first-year chit. Anyway he was tired and didn't really approve of the way some of his kind used the red females. "No," he said, and went into the drey, followed by a disappointed Gabbro. In fact, he was not happy about the way most of the younger squirrels of his kind behaved nowadays. Since the change of leadership back at Woburn, all the old moral standards seemed to have been thrown out of the trees. Okay, he'd been a bit of a lad in his time, maybe even sired a litter or two, but now – now anyone mated with anyone, at any time and in any place! He shuddered.

He shelled and ate a nut and thought of the natives they had just met. He knew what would happen now. They would hold a Council Meeting. First there would be a discussion on who these strangers were and where they came from, then demands from some that they be sent on their way.

Others, however, would want to hear what he had to say and finally there would be a decision to hear him out and, if they didn't like what he said, they would ask the two of them to leave the area. But by then he would have sown the demoralising seeds, and when the Silver Tide reached Purbeck the Reds would be swept away easily.

And so it was. Old Burdock the Tagger, still upset at what she considered to have been shabby treatment, was all for sending them on at once. But the phrase that Marble had used, "the other natives who *inhabited* the middle lands", had stuck in her mind and she felt she needed to know more. Also she had to agree that, as hospitality had been offered, it could not now be withdrawn.

> *All passing strangers*
> *Must be accommodated*
> *At whatever cost.*

Most of the demesne, especially the younger ones, were intrigued by the talk of 'numbers' and 'Stone force' and wanted to hear more. The decision reached was exactly as Marble had predicted. He was already asleep.

Chapter 4

A fox wandered under the pine trees of Steepbank as the sun peered over the distant horizon. Fingers of pale light had touched Poole Harbour away to the east, making the colours of the anchored boats glow and reflect in the water. Then these same rays, reaching westwards, lit up Brownsea and Furzey Islands, the Goathorn Peninsula, Middlebere and the Great Heath.

At the Blue Pool the light touched the tops of the tallest pines and the squirrels stirred in their warm dreys, most anticipating an exciting day learning the power of numbers that the stranger had promised to tell them. What could that be?

Below, the pool was still in darkness, the fox could smell squirrels all about but knew that they were out of his reach. He scent-marked an anthill and moved away towards Humanside. Sometimes there were scraps of Man-food to be found near the Man-earths. If not, he would trot along the deserted road to see if any rabbits had been killed there in the night. Anything for an easy life.

A pair of jays screeched with the sound of tearing linen to express their displeasure as he passed through what they considered to be *their* territory.

As the light grew stronger and the sun cleared the pine trees of Deepend, the pool began to change colour from a soft green to a deep blue, mirroring the sky. Wraiths of mist twisted over the surface and vanished. A moorhen called to her young and paddled out from under an overhanging bush, followed by five tiny black chicks pecking at insects on the surface, ripples from their frantic activity disturbing the still water. The fox looked down from the bank, sniffed the air disdainfully, having found nothing near the waste-bins; thought to himself that, if there had been, it probably wouldn't have been worth eating anyway, and slipped away towards the road.

Oak poked his head out of the drey, which was built from a mass of carefully intertwined twigs, honeysuckle bines and leaves in a fork of the Council Tree. He sniffed the air, smelt fox, the scent too faint now to inspire the paralysing fox-dread, looked carefully down, whiskers twitching to sense air movement, sniffed again to judge exactly how long it had been since the fox had left, then pulled his head back into the drey. Fern was curled up in the warm lining of moss, feathers and rabbit fur, still half asleep.

"Been a dog-fox through but he's gone now. It's going to be another hot day. We've got to listen to that grey fellow soon so you'd better stir yourself, Fern-Mate. I'm going down for a bite."

He went head-first down the scaly tree trunk, pausing now and then to look around for anything unusual, any pattern that was unfamiliar, any shape that was different from the night before, anything which could spell danger to him and his community.

"Sun, that fox stinks!"

26

Moving away from the urine-sprinkled anthill, he searched for early fungi and was soon joined by others from Beachend and Deepend. Even Juniper and Bluebell, the Scavengers, had arrived from Humanside to hear the words of the grey strangers.

Fern had followed Oak out of the drey on to her look-about branch and was grooming herself in the sunshine. She wanted to be extra smart today, with visitors there, and it was up to her to set an example. Some of those youngsters had no sense of what was important! She combed through her fur with her claws, fluffed out her tail and felt her ears. No tufts yet – hurry up, winter!

Marble watched the activity through the entrance to the Strangers' Drey, which he had found cramped and smaller than those his kind built. He was invisible to those outside, and he waited until he judged the time was exactly right.

"Now," he said, then exploded through the entrance hole and swung down through the branches of the tree, followed closely by Gabbro, frightening the Reds on the ground and causing them to freeze, then scatter and instinctively leap for the safety of the nearest tree trunk. He dropped to the ground and bounded up on to a stump in the centre of the clearing, Gabbro staying on the pine-needle-littered earth nearby. The smell of fox was strong but Marble ignored it. He had watched that animal pass underneath him an hour ago and it would be far away by now. The scent would unsettle these stupid natives and make them more susceptible.

The Reds came down out of the trees and approached the stump, glancing around warily. Oak looked up at Marble and greeted him, thought briefly of climbing on to the

27

stump himself, but he felt he needed to keep a suitable space between him and the grey creature, as otherwise it might appear that he was endorsing what the Grey might say. On the other hand it gave Marble an increase in stature to be above him. This stranger was no fool! He thought of the Kernel:

> Let others look up
> To see where the Leaders are.
> Reach down to help them.

When the chattering had died down, Marble stood on his hind legs so that he looked even more dominant.

"Form a circle," he commanded. The Reds jostled and nudged each other into a ring around him.

"Today," said Marble loudly, "I will show you some of our Ways. I will begin with numbers. It is this knowledge of numbers that makes our kind so superior." He raised his tail proudly. Oak resented this remark and glanced at Old Burdock who was clearly fuming.

The Grey looked round. "Bright Marguerite, take some dreylings and collect 'lots' of stones and bring them to me."

Marguerite skipped away, proud to have been selected and named in front of the others. With other young squirrels she found a number of stones which they rolled and carried into the circle.

Then, watched in silence by the Reds, Gabbro selected four stones of equal size and laid them out in a square on the ground. He placed a forepaw on one of the stones. Oak noticed at once that all the wood-ants foraging nearby scurried from the square in confusion.

"That is the smallest square," said Marble. "It has the number Four which you know. It has a little Power, but not much. We show it as a symbol like this." He nodded to Gabbro who then put a twig on the ground near the square with two small pine cones next to it.

The Reds tried to understand what he meant but with little success. Larch the Curious and Chestnut the Doubter climbed up into the branches above to get a clearer view.

Gabbro selected more stones and made a square with four rows of four stones. Marble said, "We symbolise this so." Gabbro added another two cones to his symbols.

The audience was mystified. They watched him pull a piece of dead bark from the tree stump, select a large black beetle from it, drop it into the square and stand with a forepaw on one of the corner stones. The beetle, which had been scrambling away, stiffened, and rolled over on to its back. Its legs contracted slowly, and it died.

"Power," said Marble, "Power." His tail rose but no one noticed, their attention was directed to the stones and the dead beetle. Gabbro's paw was still on the corner stone. Oak reached out to disturb the arrangement of the stones. He did not like this, it felt unnatural. As his paw neared the square his claws tingled and itched, and his whiskers

*Humans would call this sixteen in binary.

vibrated painfully. Then his muscles locked with cramp and he could not move.

"Stay quite still," Marble said to Oak in a commanding voice. Oak was unable to do anything else and realised that the stranger must appear to be able to command obedience from him, the Leader.

In the silence that followed there was a thump, then another. Larch and Chestnut had fallen from the tree to the ground, unconscious.

The squirrels backed away from the square of stones. Oak stayed where he was, still unable to move.

He remained there, as if petrified, for a full minute. Then Marble motioned to Gabbro who suddenly lifted his paw and scattered the stones. Oak unfroze, and the natives chattered in relief.

"If you think this is powerful you should see the effect of a square this size." He added another two cones to the line.

 *

Oak advanced stiffly on Marble. "We do not care for your Ways, Marble the Stranger, and request that you and your companion leave at once."

"As you wish, Cautious Oak," said Marble with the hint of a sneer in his voice. "But remember what you have seen when the Silver Tide comes."

Holding their tails high and twitching them insultingly, the two Greys left, heading back the way they had come. The seeds of demoralisation had been sown!

*Humans' binary sixty-four.

Chapter 5

The sound of the gates opening rang across the pool but instead of dispersing as usual, the squirrels sat in small groups in the trees, discussing the disturbing events they had just seen.

"What was the Power in the stones?"

"What is the Silver Tide?"

"When will it come, whatever it is?"

Oak felt it to be his duty to rally the squirrels and dispel this foolish talk, but he was stiff and sore and his mind was in a turmoil. The roots of his whiskers hurt. The Reds looked towards him for leadership and explanations but, when none was forthcoming, they drifted away, puzzled and dispirited.

Warily, Oak picked up one of the stones and examined it closely. Just an ordinary stone. He thought of remaking the square pattern, then dismissed the idea, it was all so unnatural. After scattering the cones that Gabbro had laid out in the line next to the twig, he climbed slowly and painfully back up to the security of his drey.

Unknown danger near –
Lie high, wait, watch and look out.
Trust in the Sun's light.

None of the squirrels noticed that young Marguerite was not in any of the groups. Even the normally sharp-eyed Burdock was somewhat befuddled by the pace of events in what was usually a quiet and perhaps even a dull demesne, and had not seen the youngster leave to follow the Greys. The old Tagger had felt portents of doom and had returned to her own drey to dredge her mind for appropriate Kernels to encourage and support her companions.

The Greys had left along one of the ground-paths and, once she was out of sight of the others, Marguerite took to the trees and raced along, jumping even quite wide gaps in her efforts to catch up with them. These strangers had some special knowledge that had created a great curiosity in her. If she didn't see them again, the chance of satisfying it might be gone for ever.

Marble heard the rustling in the branches above and behind him and waited, Gabbro silent at his side. Marguerite dropped to the ground near them, breathless.

"Excuse me, sir," she panted.

Marble held up his paw. "Wait, there is no hurry. We have all day." His face was stern yet Marguerite was aware of just a trace of warmth in his voice. She held her tail low, as was fitting for a youngster addressing a senior.

"Please, sir," she said at last, "I would like to know more about the numbers."

"What about them, Bright Marguerite?"

"Are there any numbers after eight?"

Marble looked at Gabbro. This is a bold one, he thought. Most natives are terrified when they have seen the Power demonstration and here's one wanting to know about numbers!

"Show me eight," said Marble.

She held up both paws, extending her claws.

"Show me again," said Marble.

Marguerite repeated the action.

"So there must be, Bright One," said Marble, turning away and signalling to Gabbro to follow. He wanted confusion behind him, not understanding. Understanding would give power where it was not desirable.

Marguerite stood on the path, mystified, tail low, wondering if they were laughing at her, before creeping back unnoticed to join the other unhappy Reds.

Whilst all this was taking place at the Blue Pool, Rowan the Bold had woken and stretched his stiff limbs, one by one. His fur was bejewelled with dew in the first rays of the sun. He shook himself and looked out over the water below the tree where he had slept. Down at the Eyeland end of the pool a heron was wading in the shallows, stabbing at an occasional frog. No danger about; if there had been, the heron would have been off at once with a harsh squawk and a sweep of those huge grey wings. No dragonflies were active yet, they needed sunshine to loosen up their wings after the chill of the night.

As Rowan made his way down the tree trunk, the heron paused at the sight of movement, then resumed its feeding, satisfied that the little animal on the tree at the other end of the pool was not dangerous – for the present. Rowan fed slowly, enjoying the increasing warmth as the sun rose higher and the rays lit up the trees on the Eyeland. In the mellow light, they formed a pleasing group and he felt a great urge to experience them and feel their crisp bark under his claws, and so, watched by the wary heron, he made his way along the shoreline towards that end of the pool. Finally the tall grey bird decided that perhaps the Swamp was a better place to be and flapped away out of sight, legs trailing behind him.

Rowan half circled the pool before realising, what he later told himself he had known all along, that unless he could fly like the heron, the Eyeland and those tempting trees were out of his reach. No thought of swimming had entered his head; water to a squirrel was as alien an element as the treetops would be to a mole. Eventually he gave up the dream and, with one last look at the pool where the great pink and white water-flowers were beginning to open, he turned towards the sun and home.

Chapter 6

It was early evening when Rowan, tired but elated, crossed the unmarked boundary of his home demesne. As he did so he was aware that something had changed. There was tension in the air, a foreboding of change, unwelcome change. He climbed slowly up to his parents' drey but before reaching it met his younger sister, Marguerite. She greeted him warmly.

"We've got so much to tell you, Rowan," she said. "You'll never guess who was here today!"

Rowan was full of his own news. It was customary for a squirrel returning from climbabout to be the centre of attention, as others asked about the world beyond their trees. Now, even as his parents came out to greet him, he could see that their minds were on other things.

"Rowan-Son," Oak called down to him, "welcome home. We've had some odd visitors here. Come up and we'll tell you."

Rowan decided that it was not the time to relate his adventures and listened to a recital of the events of that morning.

"Did you see any of the grey creatures?" asked Oak. He could not yet bring himself to call them squirrels.

Rowan shook his head. "I met some friendly red ones like us over beyond Screech Hill, where the barn owls live, Oak-Pa," he replied, "but none like those you say were here."

Marguerite wanted to tell him about her later meeting with the Greys but decided to leave that for another time and they sat comfortably side by side, brother and sister together again, watching the sun go down. They were still sitting there enjoying each other's company long after their parents had withdrawn into the drey for the night.

Eventually Marguerite said, "I like numbers," hoping for an interested response, but her brother's thoughts were concentrated on how to get across the water to an Eyeland surrounded by pink and white water-flowers, and he did not reply. As the moon rose they joined Oak and Fern in their drey.

As they entered, their mother started to tell of her plans for building a new drey so that the youngsters could take over this old one, but Oak cut her short.

"We can discuss that again, Fern-Mate," he said. "I'm trying to work out what all this business with the grey creatures could mean for us."

The visit of the Greys was the main topic of conversation in each of the dreys around the pool.

Juniper and Bluebell, the Scavengers, in their home high in an oak tree on Humanside, were not too concerned. They had gone to the Man-dreys after the Greys had left and had done their usual begging routine for the Visitors. Lots of food-bits had come their way, thrown from the tables on the terrace, and a good number of their favourite salted peanuts. Life was good, life was easy, tomorrow there was bound to be more.

"What did you make of those grey fellows, Bluebell-Mate?" Juniper asked sleepily.

"Here yesterday, gone today. Don't suppose we'll see them again. Did you bring any peanuts up with you; the salty ones?"

At Deepend, Chestnut the Doubter was trying to recall exactly what he had seen before he fell from the tree.

"What was the name of that Grey, the senior one, Heather-Mate?" he asked.

"Marble. Funny sort of name, I thought."

"Probably not his real name, wouldn't trust him for a minute," said Chestnut.

"I didn't like him either, arrogant sort of character, no breeding," Heather Treetops agreed. "Glad they've moved on. What do you make of this Silver Tide business?"

"Unbelievable!" Chestnut replied.

In the Beachend drey Clover the Carer was more concerned.

"Larch-Mate," she asked, "what did it feel like before you dropped out of the tree?"

She had attended to Larch the Curious and to Chestnut after the Greys had gone. It had been some time before either of them was fully conscious again and Oak had clearly not been himself after that funny business with the square of stones. She needed to know more in case something similar should happen in the future. As Carer for the community it was her task to provide relief and comfort when squirrels were not fully fit and well.

"All I remember," Larch replied, "was looking down with Chestnut and seeing that Marble fellow put his paw on one of the corner stones. Then a sort of wave hit me, coming upwards from the stones. My whiskers hurt like crazy, then I can't remember any more until I woke up with you licking my face. I'd like to know just what caused it. I still feel sick."

"Try nibbling this, Larch-Mate mine," said Clover, reaching into the mossy lining of the drey and pulling out a pawful of a sweet-scented herb. "That might help." She passed it to Larch, trying not to wake their dreyling, Tansy Quick-Thought.

The following day dawned with the same clear sky and promise of heat to come, and a brilliant sun shone down with growing intensity throughout the long morning and early afternoon.

The squirrels dozed or slept through the time of greatest heat, most of them forgetting briefly their worries about the Silver Tide, ignoring the constant passing of humans on the paths below, and only rousing themselves to feed when they heard the big gates close.

"Come and look at this," called Tansy to Rowan. "What in the name of the Sun is it?"

Below, a large red rubber beachball, left by a visiting child, was lying in a hollow below a tree. Rowan the Bold climbed down for a closer look.

"It smells like the scent Visitors' feet leave on the paths," he called up. "But I don't think it's alive." He poked it with a forepaw. The ball moved slightly and he jumped back.

The other young squirrels came down and joined him in

pushing it about, watched from above by the older ones, some of whom were still uneasy after the visit of the Greys. Was *this* something to do with the Silver Tide? What was it?

Old Burdock looked at the round red thing, thought how much it looked like the Sun and was about to call to the others to show respect, when Rowan, living up to his tag, climbed the tree, ran on to a branch, dropped on to the top of the ball and bounced into the air to land several feet away, to the amusement of the other youngsters. Then they were all at it. Squirrels racing up the tree trunk, out along the branch and dropping on to the ball, grinning and chattering with excitement at this new game.

Squirrelation took over, the infectious revelry enticing all the squirrels of the demesne to join in the fun.

The Scavengers from Humanside hopped over and, before long, with the exception of Burdock, who watched apprehensively, even the staidest of the elders were enjoying the sport.

No squirrel ever admitted to being the one who had aimed badly and, in an attempt to stay on top, had dug its claws into the red skin. Each subsequently blamed another but shortly afterwards the ball sagged and, with a gentle hiss and a sigh, "died" in a circle of contrite red squirrels. The game was over.

Later, the caretaker, on his litter round, picked up the deflated ball and stuffed it in his bag with the other rubbish, watched by the squirrels peering down from behind a screen of pine needles.

Great anvils of cumulus clouds had been building up during the early evening and now towered in the western sky, and although the setting sun was hidden, the oppressive heat remained. The squirrels were listless and uncomfortable.

> *A storm with thunder*
> *Follows three hot summer days –*
> *Then clear air again.*

So ran the old Kernel. But it had been "lots" more than three days of unusual heat. Burdock wished the storm would come soon.

Oak visited her drey to ask about the red thing that had looked like a Sun.

"It can't have been the Sun down here," she said to Oak. "That was still in the sky when I first saw it."

"It was round and red just like the Sun," replied Oak. "Smaller, though, perhaps it's the Sun's child. Does the Sun have youngsters?"

"I don't know, but it *was* like a little Sun. Why would it come here?"

"Maybe it was about to tell us before we caught squirrelation and some Sun-damned dreyling scratched it and it died."

"We won't ever know now," Burdock said slowly, dredging an old saying up from deep in her memory.

> *The Sun will prevail.*
> *Greyness eliminated then.*
> *Even a little Sun.*

"I never knew what that meant. Do you think the Greyness could be referring to those grey animals that were here yesterday? And that round thing could have been 'a little Sun'?"

"Perhaps you're right," Oak replied, with his usual caution. "It was just like a little Sun."

Burdock said hopefully, "Maybe the Sun sent its youngster to tell us not to take any notice of the Grey Ones."

"Maybe," said Oak, mentally clutching at a leaf.

The squirrels drifted apart to forage, each occupied by their own thoughts and fears. Only a pensive Juniper knew whose claws had done the fatal act.

The storm, so long in coming, broke over the Great Heath soon after nightfall, the wind raging in the tops of the pine and fir trees, whistling through the needles and penetrating into the usually cosy, warm centres of the dreys to chill the uneasy squirrels huddled inside. Flashes of lightning tore open the night sky, each branch silhouetted blackly against the intense light beyond. Squalls of rain lashed the heather and churned the surfaces of the pool into a confused mass of rings, ripples and bouncing droplets.

By morning a new Kernel was circulating, though none could say where it had originated.

> *The Sun sent its child*
> *To protect us from the Greys –*
> *And we all killed it.*

The Sun's-child Legend had been born, sending a sense of collective guilt throughout the community.

Chapter 7

When the sun rose the next day over the damp and storm-damaged woodland, causing the bracken and pine needles on the ground to steam in the early rays, a group of bedraggled red squirrels, who had obviously spent the night without proper shelter, appeared at Humanside and asked the resident guardians of that area, Juniper and Bluebell, for permission to pass through.

Throughout the morning "lots" more squirrels appeared, some singly, some in couples and some in small family groups. Most bore bite-marks on their legs, some had patches of fur missing and many were limping, unable to leap from tree to tree and having to travel, fearfully, on the ground.

They were all escorted by Juniper and Bluebell to meet Oak and Burdock, to whom they told harrowing tales of their homes being taken over by advancing waves of Greys calling themselves the Silver Tide and claiming possession of whichever areas took their fancy. Any Reds who resisted had been savaged and harassed until they gave way to the larger and more aggressive invaders.

Oak offered hospitality to the refugees but they would

not stay and, after sharing a quick meal, they moved on westwards, urging the locals to get out before it was too late.

"Leave while you can, they'll be coming here soon, Oak-Friend."

Oak replied that he and his community had been Guardians of the Blue Pool for longer than any squirrel could remember and he could not desert his trust. He would talk with the Greys when they came and ask them to move on and look for uninhabited territory to settle in.

"They won't listen," he was told. "They just take what they want. You mustn't stay. Come with us while you can. Didn't you have a visit from some missionaries?"

"Do you mean the two who showed us what they called Stone force?"

"There are lots of missionaries, they all use different methods. The ones who came to us told us all about the Sunless Pit and how we would all go there if we didn't obey their instructions. When we said we didn't believe them, they attacked us with their teeth."

Oak and Old Burdock conferred and decided that the threat had probably been exaggerated and that it was their duty to remain at the pool.

> *A Guardianship*
> *Means responsibility.*
> *Defend at all cost.*

Oak, however, remembering the effect of Marble's Power Squares on him, was apprehensive, and he was relieved when night fell with no further alarms.

Early next morning another party of "lots" of squirrels arrived and were offered hospitality. Their Leader, Alder, had a broken tail, the result of a "lesson" from a Grey.

With the exception of Bluebell and Juniper, who were entertaining the human Visitors, all the squirrel community gathered to greet and assist the refugees.

Clover looked at the mud-caked remains of Alder's broken tail, which was obviously causing him considerable pain as it dragged along the ground, his suffering evident in his drawn features and the way he winced whenever he moved his rump.

"That's going to have to come off, Alder-Friend," she said gently, "or it will go bad. Would you like me to do it?"

Alder considered for a moment. A squirrel without a tail would feel like half a squirrel, but his tail was worse than useless as it was, and without it he could lead his party away from the danger faster.

"Yes, please do, but spare my whiskers," he said, trying to make a joke of it. A tail is important to a squirrel but without whiskers one becomes a bumbling idiot.

Clover passed him a large pine cone. "Hug this," she told him. "Shut your eyes and count to eight."

Alder gripped the cone and started to count. At "two" Clover severed the tail quickly and cleanly with a single bite. Alder hardly felt a thing and went on counting, "three, four, five . . . "

"Works every time," said Clover, slipping away to bury the scraggy tail in a disused rabbit hole.

When she came back, Alder, surrounded by the rest of his party, was licking away the blood oozing from the stump. His life-mate, Dandelion, whose skin had several

44

bald patches and the signs of recent scars, was comforting him.

"It'll stop bleeding soon," Clover told Alder, "but lick it clean several times each day and I'll give you something to put on it. Now you must rest."

A youngster, Tamarisk, already tagged the Tactless, kept asking Clover what she had done with Alder's tail, until Heather led him away.

Alder wanted to press on with his group, but Clover and Dandelion persuaded him to stay for at least half a day and to make the others with him rest too.

"He'll get the shivers in a few minutes," Clover told them. "We must help him to the Strangers' Drey."

Dandelion took charge and, despite Alder's protests, led him away to rest.

Clover slipped off to find a plant of woundwort, whose healing properties had been known to Caring squirrels since the days of the first squirrels in the world, Acorn and Primrose.

Rowan had been watching one of the younger female squirrels, a yearling like himself. She seemed not to have a mate with her and was looking tired and forlorn. He introduced himself. "I'm Rowan the Bold."

"You are that," she said, smiling. "I'm Meadowsweet. Alder is my father."

Rowan asked about their journey and their home Guardianship. "It is ... it was, a place called Wolves-barrow, Rowan-Friend," she told him. "We've been following the Leylines."

Rowan briefly wondered what a Leyline was, but was more interested in the fascinating way she twitched her whiskers at him and used her paws and tail to emphasise what she was saying. This is a very special squirrel, he thought to himself and, to prolong their meeting, he took her to view the pool. He thought that he had never seen a squirrel leap with such style and grace.

Later, returning to the rest of the group, she thanked him. "I really forgot our situation for a few hours," she said. "I feel much stronger. We are leaving now – I must go and help my father. Perhaps we shall meet again some day."

"I hope so, Meadowsweet-Friend," said Rowan.

Rowan sat on a high branch, eyes moist with the tears that squirrels cannot shed, flicking the "fond farewell" signal with his tail. So engrossed was she with her father that Meadowsweet did not look back until the very last minute before they disappeared from sight. Although by then they were a long way apart, Rowan was sure that she returned his signal and he turned sadly away. He would have followed had he not felt that he was needed here at the Blue Pool.

That night he dreamt of living on a beautiful Eyeland in a lovely pool with an even lovelier Meadowsweet beside him as his life-mate.

Love conquered duty.

At first light he left without even telling his sister or his parents of his intentions, and hurried off in the direction of the Clay-Pan, only to find that a shower in the night had washed away any traces of footprints or scent. By High Sun he was forced to give up the search and return to his family.

If only I'd asked about those Leylines, I might know which direction they had taken, he thought ruefully.

Chapter 8

Over the course of the next three days the flow of refugees slowed to a trickle, then died to nothing at about the time of High Sun on the third day. Late that afternoon, just after the last of the human Visitors had left, the first squirrels of the Silver Tide arrived at the Blue Pool Demesne.

Two male and two female Greys appeared at Humanside, found Juniper the Scavenger living up to his tag, and demanded that he take them to see the Senior Squirrel. With arrant discourtesy they marched through the Humanside, Deepend and Steepbank Guardianships, tails high, ignoring the watching natives as they followed Juniper to where Oak was waiting, warned by the turmoil in the community that something was amiss.

Oak greeted them formally.

The male Greys introduced themselves as Flint and Quartz, the females as Chert and Granite. Oak thought that the foursome looked as hard as their names sounded.

"We have come to arrange territories for our use," said Flint.

"I'm sorry but this demesne is fully guardianed," said Oak. "You must seek elsewhere."

"I said – we have come to arrange territories for our own use," repeated Flint, slowly. "Marble, the missionary whom you have met, has told us that the humans' side of the pool would be very suitable. We'll take that. From now on it will be known as New Connecticut."

The four Greys left, tails high.

Oak was bemused and angry. Nothing in his experience, nor in any of the Kernels he could recall, fitted this situation. He followed the Greys to protest, but they were gone, heading in a group back through Deepend, watched from a distance by other anxious Reds.

On reaching Humanside the Greys located the guardians' drey in the oak tree and destroyed it twig by twig, ignoring the furious protests of Juniper and Bluebell. The four built two new dreys in a beech tree nearby and one pair moved into each.

Juniper and Bluebell spent a cold night in the open, watching, until the Greys emerged at dawn to forage on the ground. It was then that Juniper, his tail raised defiantly, climbed the beech tree on the side away from the Greys and began to dismantle one of their dreys, throwing the twigs to the ground.

His gesture did not go unnoticed for long.

Together the four Greys climbed the smooth-barked trunk and surrounded him, then just sat staring at him as though he was the slimiest piece of fox-dropping ever seen. Soon his tail sagged and hung limply over the branch on which he sat.

Flint lunged at him and he drew back startled, only to flinch again as Quartz made a similar move from his other side. "Look out, Brown Job," called a female voice from behind him and he turned to face Chert, who crept forward menacingly, then sat grinning at him.

Juniper looked around desperately for a way of escape, saw a chance and dropped on to a branch below. Quartz and Chert followed. He ran along a limb and leapt into the next tree, then the next and the next, the Greys effortlessly staying a few squirrel-lengths behind him.

In his anxiety to escape, Juniper did not plan his route and, perhaps because he was looking over his shoulder frequently, he found he was back in the tree from which he had started, face to face with Flint and Granite. Every breath was hurting him and there was a painful pounding in his chest.

He turned along a side branch and leapt into another tree. When he next looked over his shoulder there were the faces of the two rested Greys close behind. He caught a glimpse of Quartz and Chert sitting in the beech tree, grinning as they watched the chase.

Juniper was tiring rapidly and making ill-judged leaps, but the Greys seemed in no hurry to catch up with him. His progress became more and more clumsy and soon he was having to pause before each leap to gather his breath, while the Greys also paused and called insulting remarks at him. He leapt again and realised that once more he was back in the beech tree.

Quartz ran at him and he lost his hold and fell to the ground with a bone-shaking impact, too tired to turn gracefully in the air as he would normally have done.

Sick and tired, he lay there panting and terrified as all the Greys came down the trunk head-first, sneering at him.

"We're not finished with you yet, Brown Job," Flint

hissed in his face. "Get up and run." He nipped the exhausted squirrel's tail painfully.

"Now. Run, I said!" He nipped again.

Juniper ran, the Greys keeping pace on either side of him, nipping at his legs and tail. The harassment continued, his retreat being cleverly guided along the ground under low bushes towards a tall tree, its upper branches overhanging the pool.

Here the Greys allowed him to climb before following, biting at his tail and forcing him ever further out along a branch which spread over the water.

Juniper turned to face his tormentors but was driven back down the thinning branch in mounting terror.

An uncontrolled fall and deep water are two of the things a squirrel fears most.

The Greys paused to let Juniper feel the full horror of his situation. Then, slowly and deliberately, they began to gnaw at the branch, tearing off great splinters and letting them drop, to splash in the water below. Juniper hung on desperately as the bough began to sag downwards. The Greys paused again, prolonging his agony. They knew other Reds were watching and that this was to be a lesson to them all, one they would never forget.

Juniper clung to the branch, now hanging only by a strip of bark. He was paralysed by water-dread, his eyes swivelling around in terror searching for a safe place to leap to, yet knowing he had no strength to make such a leap.

Then Flint bit through the last strip of bark.

The branch fell, Juniper clinging on, chattering with fear.

Hitting the water, the branch was submerged, dragging

the squirrel down with it. Then it rose slowly to the surface. Juniper, coughing and spluttering, held tight to the wet bark, his body racked with spasms of pain, until the breeze eventually blew the branch to the shore.

He crawled on to the sandy beach, bedraggled and sodden, and lay there gasping.

The Greys went off to forage as though nothing had happened.

Later, much later, Juniper and Bluebell sought refuge with the Deependers.

"Greetings to you Chestnut the Doubter, and to you Heather Treetops," Juniper began formally. "We, Juniper and Bluebell, tagged the Scavengers, seek sanctuary in your Guardianship. As I am sure you have seen, the Greys have taken over Humanside. Temporarily," he added, with unconvincing bravado.

Chestnut looked at the forlorn squirrels on the trunk below him, then at Heather. He had no cause to doubt what he had been told, as he had witnessed the chase himself. Heather flicked her tail as if to say, "You decide if you want *these* two in our area," and went into their drey.

He looked again at the pathetic pair, pictured himself harried and homeless, and said, "Yes, my friends, choose a tree, I'll get some others and we'll help you build."

Soon, in a show of community spirit, a new and comfortable drey had been assembled in the fork of a Deepend pine, Heather herself collecting the moss for the lining, and Fern ensuring that, even if it was for the Scavengers, it was tidy and respectable.

*

That evening, an emergency Council Meeting was called.

Greetings were quick and formal and the Protection Kernel was said for the first time that most could remember.

> *Great Guardian Sun*
> *Giver of all life and warmth*
> *Protect your squirrels.*

The Bright One wondered if the Sun included grey as well as red squirrels, but did not ask.

"Do we just let them take what they want?" Heather Treetops asked scornfully.

Marguerite had once asked her mother how Heather had earned that tag.

"She is very proud of the fact that her grandfather was the last of the hereditary chiefs of this demesne and believes that places her above all of us," Fern had told her. "It is one of Old Burdock's best and truest tags. I wish I could have a new tag, I'm sure that 'the Fussy' isn't really appropriate to me."

She had smoothed her tail as she had said this and Marguerite had turned away to hide her smile.

Oak looked uncomfortable. There was a big difference between being Leader in a stable, year-to-year cycle of seasons, with comforting Kernels from a wise Tagger to guide you in decision-making, and being Leader now with unprecedented things happening in one's demesne.

"I doubt if there is anything we can do," said Chestnut and turned away to avoid the withering look his mate gave him.

Burdock intervened to cool the debate.

"We were warned what would happen by the other squirrels who passed through here, though some of us didn't believe them." She glanced at Chestnut. "Or didn't want to."

> *Avoid illusions.*
> *Reality must be faced.*
> *Be down-to-earth now.*

Marguerite played with the words. She knew that squirrels were at home in the trees and that down-to-earth was what Old Burdock had taught her was a figure of speech, but it was so easy up in the branches to lose sight of all the things going on below in a world which did affect them, even if they sometimes felt above it all.

Larch was speaking now. "I wonder what it is they want. Are they intending to stay here? Will there be more of them? Will they want to take more of what they called territory?"

Oak held up his paw. "One question at a time. But none of us knows the answers anyway. Time will tell us more."

> *If mists hide the view*
> *All will be revealed to us,*
> *In the Sun's good time.*

Finally, a decision was taken to abandon Humanside to the Greys, in the hope that they would be content there. Juniper and Bluebell were given permission to stay on at Deepend. Then Juniper, realising that the easy pickings from the Visitors would not be his that summer, asked if he could have a new tag.

Old Burdock the Tagger looked at him coldly. "The one that comes to mind is Juniper the Diver. Would you like that?"

This raised the only laugh of the day. Juniper turned away. Any new tag would have to be earned.

Chapter 9

Seven days and nights had passed since the Greys had arrived. Marguerite had watched the event, especially the humiliation of Juniper, with interest. Now well grown, she was living up to the early promise that Burdock had recognised. The tag she had been given, the Bright One, was ambiguous. She puzzled over it and wondered if it referred to her glossy brown fur or her eyes. Or was it because she seemed to understand complicated things better than others of her year? It was against custom to ask about your tag, as this would be an insult to the wisdom and observation of the Tagger.

Now she was concerned as to how only four Greys, admittedly bigger physically than the natives, could intimidate a group of squirrels who outnumbered them many times over.

Bluebell was concerned about far more mundane things, like how to get some of the salted peanuts she craved. She hung about the edge of Humanside watching the Greys scavenging at the Tea Rooms, which they called the Eating Man-Drey. Each day she ventured nearer, apparently unnoticed, until one day a peanut, sparkling with salt, thrown by a Visitor, rolled past the Greys towards her. She ran forward, grabbed at the nut and dashed away with it, not daring to look back in case the dreaded Greys were coming after her.

Safely back at Deepend she ate the peanut slowly, relishing the exquisite saltiness. She was hooked. She must have more, whatever the dangers. Early the next morning, before the human Visitors arrived, she returned, planning to be hidden ready to be the first to have any salted nuts that day.

As she came down a tree near the Eating Man-Drey and was about to drop over the bank behind the buildings she saw Flint, apparently waiting for her. She turned to avoid him, her whiskers twitching nervously, and thought of running back towards Deepend. Then a harsh screech sounded from above her and a grey body dropped from a branch.

She instinctively jumped sideways and Quartz landed where she had been a moment before.

"Missed you that time," he said, striking out at her with his paw.

Bluebell, terrified, leapt away and scampered off through the trees, pursued by the mocking laughter of the two Greys.

When she realised that she was not actually being chased, she slowed to a hop and then stopped – the salt craving still on her! She turned; there was no sign of the Greys now and she started back again. Near the Man-dreys she heard the mocking laughter again, but could not make out where it was coming from. Cones were dropped on her and mysterious rustlings came from the bushes, but no squirrel seemed to be there.

Her fur stood on end when a stone rolled down the bank and she had to jump clear. Then she found a square of four stones where she knew none had been a few moments before.

Only the salt craving held her – every instinct told her to climb and run through the treetops to safety. She kept telling herself that it could only be Flint and Quartz playing tricks to scare her and she hesitatingly called their names, "Flint, Quartz, please. I only want some nuts!"

Mocking laughter came from above and behind her, but she could not see her tomentors. Then, hearing the clang of the metal gates being opened, she scampered down the bank and into the area in front of the Eating Man-Drey, confident that the presence of humans would protect her. She stayed in the open, waiting for Visitors to arrive and be brought their food by the Red- Haired Girl, other Greys arriving and also waiting expectantly. Flint and Quartz were amongst them, leering at her and bumping into her as they scurried about.

Then she saw it. A peanut, salt-encrusted, was thrown to her. She caught it, dropped it, then ran after it as it bounced down the steps towards the pool. She caught it again and sat up breathlessly, holding the nut, only to be bowled over by Flint who had bounded down the steps behind her. The nut flew from her paws, bouncing and rolling, to splash in the water.

By the time she had evaded Flint and scooped the nut from the shallow water, it had lost its appeal and tasted like the other peanuts which were more easily begged from the Visitors.

She waited all day, enduring the threats and abuse from

the Greys until, when the last Visitor had left, she scurried away and ran back to Deepend and the security of her drey.

Juniper had missed her, knew that she had been at Humanside and guessed that she had been overcome by the salt craving. It took *him* sometimes, and he knew how hard he had to fight within himself to resist it.

He decided not to speak of it that night. He could explain how he could help her in the morning, when she would be calmer. They slept restlessly together, but while he was still asleep she slipped away from the drey and although he searched until the gates clanged he could not find her. Then he saw her near the Man-dreys submitting to every kind of abuse from the Greys.

Bluebell returned to the drey that night, but refused to speak to Juniper about what he had seen.

She was gone again in the morning and it was inevitable that a report on her behaviour reached Old Burdock. To Juniper's disgrace, as well as her own, she was summoned to appear before the Council and account for her behaviour.

She told how she *needed* the salty nuts and could only get them at the Eating Man-Drey. Yes, the Greys did treat her badly, but she *must* have the salted nuts. Bluebell could not lie, she did not know what a lie was, but she made the various incidents of abuse and humiliation seem almost routine.

No member of the Council could conceive of the idea of an urge so irresistible that it would lead a squirrel into such behaviour, except perhaps Juniper, who remembered the taste from his scavenging days. His mouth watered at the recollection.

A denigratory tag was clearly justified and Burdock thought long and hard for a suitable one, hampered by a lack of words for such an alien action. Bluebell was sent out of listening distance during the discussions. Then, after much debate, she was called back and given the down-tag Who Sells Herself for Peanuts, and with this she crept away from the Council in disgrace, tail low.

Juniper tried to follow but she turned on him, snapping, "Leave me alone," and later, when he expected to find her at their drey, she was not there and did not return. She had gone to Humanside to live amongst the Greys, totally dependent on a supply of the salt-encrusted nuts.

Chapter 10

Some days later, Bluebell watched the arrival of another
posse of Greys which included a confident male whom she
recognised as Marble. He was accompanied by his
companion Gabbro, whom she remembered as having
been strangely silent on the last visit but now chattered
constantly.

Marble showed his surprise at finding a Red living
among the Greys and greeted her curtly but, as the salt-
dominated days passed, she was relieved to find that he
always treated her in a civil enough way. By picking up
snatches of the Greys' conversation she learned that
Marble had guided this group of colonisers to the Blue Pool
and was resting there for a time before returning to
Woburn, where it was hinted that he had great expecta-
tions. She noted that he was frequently accompanied by a
grey female known as Sandstone and once or twice she
overheard him address her affectionately as Sandy.

One afternoon, hearing sounds of violent conflict near
the Eating Man-Drey, Bluebell was drawn by curiosity to
climb on to the wood shingle roof and peer over. Below her,
tables were being pushed back, people were standing up,

some were shouting and one woman was slashing with a dog lead at a whirling black, white and grey mass on the floor. From her viewpoint she could see that a fight was in progress between a Visitor's Jack Russell terrier and one of the grey squirrels.

The whining dog, bitten about the nose and ears, was whipped off and dragged away towards the car park, leaving a squirrel, who she could see was Marble, unconscious on the ground. An elderly man with a kind face stooped to pick up the limp animal. Another man, whom she recognised as the Human Who Picked Things Up, shouted at him and he drew back.

This man knelt and called to the Red-Haired Girl who came out of the Tea Rooms and gave him an old towel in which he wrapped the body of Marble. He stood up, holding the squirrel, and turned to her.

"A vet should see this," he said.

"The vet's here now, over at the paddock with the horses, but I don't know if he'll bother with a squirrel. You could try," she suggested.

The caretaker went off towards the paddock, carrying the wrapped-up squirrel, and found the vet just as he was packing up to leave.

"Hello," he said cheerfully, recognising the caretaker. "What have you got there?"

"It's a grey squirrel, had a fight with a dog down by the Tea Rooms and got chewed up a bit. Helen, the waitress, said you were here so I brought it over."

"Let's see the little fellow," the vet said, reaching out to take the bundle, which was now showing blood on the white towelling. The squirrel was beginning to stir. "I'll just give him a small injection to keep him quiet while I look at him."

The vet lowered the back door of his estate car to make a platform, laid out a rubber sheet, then prepared a syringe. When he was sure that the squirrel was safely under, he cleaned the blood from its fur and examined the limp body.

"His right front paw is badly bitten, but there doesn't appear to be any other serious damage – one can't be sure, though. I'll have to take off that paw if he's going to have a chance to survive. Even then he may have internal injuries. Would you rather I put him down?"

Tom shook his head. "No, give the poor beggar a chance."

The vet reached into his bag for instruments and operated swiftly and cleanly.

"I'll be interested to know how he gets on," the vet said. "Animals can do surprisingly well with one paw missing, but sometimes the others will turn on it and drive it away. Let me know if you see it again, I'm over here quite often."

Tom cautiously rewrapped the squirrel in the towel.

"He'll be okay in a few hours," the vet told him. "I suggest you leave him in an open box to recover. When he's up to it he'll go off on his own."

Then, as he wiped and put away the instruments, he asked if the other squirrels seemed healthy. "There was an article I saw in a journal about some mysterious disease affecting grey squirrels in some parts of the country. No one knows how it is spread, but the squirrels seem to go into a decline, lose their natural resistance and then die from any small infection they would normally resist. There's research into it being done at Norwich. They're calling it Gradual Decline Syndrome, 'Grades' for short."

"The grey ones have only been here a few weeks," Tom replied. "Prefer the red ones myself, but don't see so much of them now. Except that scruffy one who's mad on peanuts."

The vet raised an inquisitive eyebrow.

Oh, yes, do anything for a peanut that one, got to be salted, though."

"Well I never," said the vet, closing the rear car door. "How many Reds are here?"

"Hard to tell," Tom replied. "About fifteen or twenty, I suppose. Can't say I've ever tried to count them."

Tom walked back to the Tea Rooms, carrying the squirrel, and found the waitress. "The vet fixed him up, but had to cut one of his paws off, and said I should leave him out in a box under the trees until he comes round."

"Poor little thing," Helen said sympathetically, and reached out to stroke the squirrel's head. Seeing the sharp teeth exposed where Marble's lips were drawn back, she paused, then turned and went to find a box.

An hour later, curious to know if it had gone, Tom went over to the box, saw the squirrel still lying there with its eyes closed, and went to pick it up for a closer look at what the vet had done. He instantly regretted this. At his touch the squirrel turned its head and sank its teeth deep into his fingers. He danced about, shaking his hand and shouting, "Let go, you little beggar, let go, damn you." Eventually Marble did so and, as fast as he could in his drugged state and with a front leg that no longer seemed to reach the ground, made for the nearest tree, trying to dodge Tom's boot as he kicked savagely at him.

"Ungrateful swine," shouted Tom at the squirrel, wrapping a dirty handkerchief around his bleeding finger.

Marble felt very sick indeed. Nauseous from the anaesthetic, with a cruel pain where his paw had been and wishing now that he had not teased the terrier, he crouched behind a tree trunk watching Tom depart, grumbling.

When Marble did eventually get back to the Man-dreys that evening after the humans had left, the other Greys crowded round sniffing and peering.

"Marble's lost one of his paws," said one, not known for his diplomacy. "Where did you see it last, Marble?"

A grey youngster, carefully keeping out of sight behind the other larger squirrels, cruelly chanted, "Marble, Three Paws," before receiving a cuff from Gabbro. The name, however, as persistent as a red squirrel's tag, was to stick to him all his life.

That same evening, across the pool, the Reds were discussing the incident involving Marble and the dog. Juniper, from his new drey in the Deepend Guardianship, had witnessed the fight. He often watched the Man-dreys, hoping that Bluebell would see him, tire of the way the Greys treated her, abandon the peanuts and come back to him.

"That dog really got him," said Juniper. "But he fought back well, no trace of hound-dread." Juniper was torn between admiration for the way a fellow squirrel, even if a grey one, had defended itself, and pleasure in having seen one of those he now blamed for Bluebell's downfall savaged.

"What happened then?" asked Oak.

"The Sun-damned Grey was lying there, not moving, and the Man Who Picks Things Up took him away. Later on I saw him put the Grey on the ground near the foot of my

64

old drey-tree in one of those things that people carry fodder in, and leave him there." Juniper was enjoying being the centre of attention, and this time not for his misde-meanours.

"What happened then?" Oak asked again.

"Nothing for a bit," said Juniper. "Then the human came back and the Grey bit him and after that he went to join the others, but was falling about and couldn't walk very well."

"Serves him right," said Heather. "Damnation to them all."

Chapter 11

Juniper lay in his drey, listening to the crackling and rustling of dead leaves as they twisted and settled into new positions. The dew which had soaked the outer leaves in the night was drying rapidly in the sunshine. He stretched luxuriously, then felt a pang of regret as he once more realised he was alone. Bluebell was somewhere away in Humanside with those grey creatures.

He was stretching himself again, guiltily enjoying the extra space, when his whiskers started to buzz and tingle painfully. He pressed them with his paws but the buzzing continued, then stopped as suddenly as it had begun. He felt a little sick.

Poking his head cautiously through the side of the drey, he looked down and counted eight Greys at the foot of the tree. He counted again. It was eight, the same number as his claws. Four he recognised, but the others were strange to him. More new arrivals? Another wave of the Silver Tide? What were they doing down there?

His queasiness increased and he had some difficulty in focusing his eyes. When his vision cleared he saw that the Greys were arranging a square of stones at the base of his tree. There were "lots" of stones, certainly more than eight. He tried to count again. For some reason, it seemed to be important to know how many stones there were.

He counted four on one side of the square and four on the other side; in fact there were four on every side. He tried to work out how many that made but still came up with the answer "lots".

The Grey, Quartz, came forward and put his forepaw on one of the corner stones. Juniper's whiskers instantly buzzed and tingled, much worse than before, and his body started to shake uncontrollably.

The Grey lifted his paw and the buzzing and shaking stopped. Juniper hung limply out of the drey coughing and retching, his head aching intolerably.

Quartz called up to him, his voice faint and distorted by the ringing in Juniper's ears. "Had enough yet, Brown Job?"

Juniper couldn't move. He felt weak and ached all over.

Again Quartz put a paw on the corner stone. The Powerwaves hit Juniper and his body contracted and shook, spasms of pain rippling along his muscles. His back arched from the invisible force and, unable to make his claws hold on, he slipped out of the entrance of the drey and fell to the ground, landing amongst the stones and scattering them, his limbs twitching feebly. The force had gone, but he was lying, limp and winded, in a circle of savage grey faces. He had never felt so bad nor so scared in his life. It was worse than the fall into the pool.

Quartz leant forward, pushing his face close to Juniper's. Even in his present position Juniper resented the intrusion. This was *his* space! He tried to draw his head back.

67

Always give others
The space they need to live in.
Squirrels respect this.

He was unable to move. The Grey pushed his face right up to Juniper's. Didn't the Grey know the Kernel?

"Listen, Brown Job," hissed Quartz, "we've had orders from the Great Lord Silver to expand this colony, so we're taking over this precinct, the one you lot call Deepend. So get out and tell the others; unless you want more Stone force, that is."

Not waiting for a reaction, he signalled to the other Greys, and together they turned and left, not one of them looking back.

Later, when he had recovered sufficiently, Juniper made his way along to the drey-tree of Chestnut the Doubter, Guardian of Deepend, and attracted his attention by scratching on the bark of the tree. He was still unfit to climb. Chestnut came down to investigate.

"Oh, it's you, Juniper the Scavenger," he said. Even now Juniper winced at the derogatory tag. "You're in a mess. Did you find yourself a bag of peanuts?"

"No," said Juniper weakly. "Some Greys came, eight of them." He twitched his front claws at Chestnut as if to validate what he was saying. "They made a pattern of stones under my drey-tree and I fell. Like *you* did when that first Grey, Marble, came. Sun, I feel bad."

"Are you sure you didn't dream it?" asked Chestnut, true to his tag. "How many did you say there were?"

"Eight. For the Sun's sake go to Steepbank to tell Oak, we're all in danger. I can't climb. I'll go down by the Little

Pool and hide. Get him to come down there, I must talk to him. Urgently!" he added, as Chestnut hung about indecisively, his mate and their two dreylings behind him. "Go now."

"Are you sure it really happened?" Chestnut asked again.

"Yes. Go *now*." Juniper turned and, stumbling and rolling in places, painfully made his way towards the Little Pool. Here he found a hiding place in a clump of rushes, glad that it was now too late in the morning for foxes to be about.

Oak was in his drey with Fern, upset and fretting because he felt aware of some serious danger but could not yet sense exactly what it was. When he heard rustling and scratching outside, he poked his head crossly out of the drey and was taken aback to find the entire Deepend family on his look-about branch.

Chestnut was flicking the "Urgent" signal with his tail.

"What is it? What has happened?" Oak asked, as Fern tried to wriggle past him through the entrance.

"Shusssh," said Chestnut, looking over his shoulder. "Danger! It's the Greys." He explained what they had done to Juniper and told Oak that the sick squirrel was hiding on the ground down by the Little Pool.

"I must go to him," Oak replied. "On the ground, you said?"

Leaders help squirrels
Regardless of the dangers.
Duty demands this.

He looked around. There was no sign of the Greys, the gate-noise hadn't come yet, so it was a safe time for him to go and find Juniper. Relatively safe, his cautious mind added.

"You lot stay here," he told the Deependers, glowering at Fern so that she knew that her place was to remain with them.

He found Juniper easily. An odd vibration emanated from his hiding place, causing Oak's whiskers to tickle gently even when he was some distance away. By turning his head from side to side he knew exactly the direction and how far from him Juniper was. It was uncanny, and unnerving, but he was soon amongst the rushes hearing the events of that morning from the sick and dishevelled squirrel.

"Oak-Leader," Juniper gasped, wanting to say "Oak-Friend" but aware, even in his present state, that over-familiarity would be resented from one with a denigratory tag. "Oak-Leader, we are in danger. The Greys are planning to take more territory. Sun, my whiskers hurt." He rubbed them with his paws as he spoke. "They're going to take over Deepend. They told me."

Oak was about to say, "Over my dead body," but checked himself, afraid that it might come to that.

"We'll see, we'll see," he said, and then went off to find Clover the Carer to ask if any of her herbs might help Juniper recover.

Chapter 12

The Guardians of Beachend, Larch and Clover, decided, with the approval of the Council, to move temporarily into the Steepbank Guardianship. They felt exposed and vulnerable so near the Greys occupying Humanside. They had noticed how more Greys were arriving every day and were foraging all through Beachend without any reference to Larch or Clover at all. If the guardians dared to approach, they were either ignored or insulted, and after the incident with Juniper they stayed well away from the intruders.

Juniper, able to climb again, although still having bouts of nausea, was living in the Strangers' Drey at Steepbank.

Chestnut and Heather, the Guardians of Deepend, had differing views on the situation. Chestnut suggested to her that they might consider following the example of Larch and Clover, and move on to Steepbank "just in case".

"Don't be such a squimp," she said. "It'll take more than a bunch of tree-rats to move *me* out of *my* home!"

"We've got our youngsters to think of," he said. "It's not just us. If there's any truth in what Juniper said about those stones it could be nasty for them. Let's see what Oak thinks."

The Council, now meeting at least once a day, decided that it would be prudent for Chestnut and Heather to build a new drey, still within their Guardianship but much closer to Steepbank.

Larch and Clover, not so brave, built near Oak and Fern's drey at Steepbank, and satisfied their Guardianship duties by making daily patrols through the Beachend treetops.

Each day the Greys encroached further, foraging far into both the Deepend and Beachend Guardianships. They had effectively taken over the hazel copse which all the Blue Pool community normally shared in the autumn. Larch and Clover were powerless to do anything other than report back to the Council.

"There are so many of them, and they are all so big," said Clover. She proposed to an early morning meeting of the Council that perhaps they should consider moving to a safer area, away from the Blue Pool altogether. "The dreylings are all strong enough for a journey now."

Larch the Curious backed her up. "All those other squirrels who came through here last moon had decided to move on. It might be exciting to explore and find a new home. I'm prepared to give it a try. The weather's good for travelling now."

Oak looked at Fern. He knew that she hated change and had just got their drey the way she had wanted it to be. "We can't just give up our Guardianships like that!"

A Guardianship
Given, is a sacred trust.
Hold and protect it.

72

"That's all very well," said Juniper. "But how can we do anything? Not only are they bigger, and there are more of them, but they know how to use those stones. And their teeth," he added.

"Can't we learn to use the stones too?"

The adults looked round to see who had spoken. It was Marguerite. "I saw how Marble did it."

"Hush, dear, while the Council is meeting," said Fern.

Youngsters were encouraged to attend Council if they wished, once they had been tagged, but were not expected to speak at meetings until after their first winter.

"I don't think we should play around with things we don't understand," said Chestnut.

"Perhaps we should just stay here and see what happens. We can leave later if we have to," Juniper said, for he was still hoping that Bluebell would give up those wretched peanuts and come back to him. Each day he ventured as far into Deepend as he dared, to watch her at the Man-dreys. Each day his hopes were dashed as he saw her humiliated and abused by Grey after Grey and watched her fawning on the Visitors at the tables.

"I agree, for now. We'll meet again this evening," said Oak, and the families dispersed.

Juniper waited until he heard the gates open, then, staying in the treetops, crossed Deepend until he was close to the Man-dreys. He was almost sure that the Greys would not dare bother him while there were Visitors about. He could see Bluebell hopping about expectantly under the tables, but then, as he watched, he heard grey-squirrel-chatter below and had to retreat to avoid being seen by a party of foraging Greys.

73

Back at Steepbank he climbed a tree to where he could look out and see the Man-dreys across the pool. He stretched out on a branch and watched, a dull ache in his chest.

The younger squirrels, aware of the tensions and uncertainties felt by the elders, stayed close to their parents' dreys, but Old Burdock still got them together once a day for their training and the recitation of the Basic Kernels that each was expected to know.

> *Ignorant squirrels*
> *Not knowing all their Kernels*
> *Will act foolishly.*

Marble's stump of a forelimb healed quickly. He had managed to climb to his drey with only one forepaw and Gabbro brought him food but no other Grey visited and he was bitterly disappointed that Sandy had also stayed away.

When he felt fit enough, he came out and carefully lowered himself backwards down the trunk, the loss of his paw hampering him considerably. He fell the last few feet to the ground and hopped over to join the other foraging Greys. Sandy was with them but although Gabbro came over at once and greeted him, Sandy kept her distance and Marble soon realised that she had transferred her affections to a large Grey with an exceptionally bushy tail and strong-looking limbs.

He approached Flint and Quartz but they continued to talk to one another as though they could not see him and, when a chit of a young Grey called out, "Marble, Three Paws," he turned and went towards the hazel copse and the

Dogleg Field. Here Gabbro helped him build a drey in a spruce tree that had once been taken indoors and used as a Christmas tree by humans, before being replanted in the woods. The disturbance had stunted the tree and it had failed to grow to its normal height, but the dense mass of twigs around the lower trunk was ideal for a three-pawed squirrel to use when it had to climb up or down.

Here Marble was to live in virtual exile, visited occasionally by Gabbro who brought news of the increasing number of Greys arriving at the Blue Pool Colony, and passing on all the news from Woburn. Marble listened with interest and when Gabbro had gone, would lie in his drey reflecting, "If only . . ."

Rowan often took his sister Marguerite on short expeditions along the "safe" side of Steepbank, teaching her the names of the plants and the trees and showing her the different creatures that shared the heath and woodlands with the squirrels. Recently, at the Little Pool, he had shown her a dragonfly larva as it crawled up a reed-stem out of the water and together they watched for an hour, any danger from Greys or foxes totally forgotten, as the ugly insect clinging to the stem split open along its back and another, apparently quite different, one climbed out of the empty case. The sun dried the four shimmering wings as they unfolded, the huge eyes brightened and the colour of its tail intensified to a brilliant blue. One by one the gaudy insect flexed its legs and tested its wings until, with a whirr and a clicking, it rose, circled over the pool and flew away, breaking the spell that had held them for so long.

They also visited the Clay-Pan, which in winter was a

shallow pool, but in summer dried out to become a favourite place for lizards to bask in the sun, the surface of the pan breaking up into hard grey-white cakes. Overhanging the greater part of the Clay-Pan was an ancient fir tree, its gnarled roots reaching into and over the bank which surrounded the pan and the trunk leaning at an angle which cast a welcome shadow when the sun was at its highest.

On one of these explorations Marguerite sat in this shade with Rowan, scratching the surface of one of the clay cakes with her claws. She was trying to explain something to him. Something that had been growing in her mind but which she could not yet formulate precisely, even to herself. Rowan indulged her, listening intently, trying to follow.

"You remember what I told you about Marble and Gabbro and the Power Squares?" she asked him.

"Yes," said Rowan, although the memory was not clear.

"Well, I think the way Marble showed the numbers with the pine cones was clumsy. What do you think of these?" She scratched some symbols on the clay.

"This is for one." She held up one claw, then pointed to a mark in the clay: 1

She indicated the angle at the top of the figure and said, "Here is a corner to hide one nut in, so this is for *one*.

"And this is for *two*: Z

"See that *two* has *two* corners. It's really quite easy. Here is *three*:" 3

Marguerite showed him 4 5 6 7 and 8

Rowan, watching a grass snake on the other side of the Clay-Pan, wasn't now giving her his full attention. What was the use of this obsession with numbers? But then, sensing how important it all seemed to his sister, he turned back and studied the scratches in the clay.

"I don't like the eight," he said. "This would be a more elegant shape and still have eight corners to hide your imaginary nuts in." He drew 4

"I like that!" said Marguerite. "It's a four with another four underneath it but upside down – eight *is* two lots of four."

"What comes after eight?" he asked. "Do you have a sign for 'lots'?"

"I haven't got that far," admitted Marguerite, "but I will soon." She scratched X to show that they were *her* marks and turned to follow her brother as he chased after a grasshopper.

Heavy clouds covered the sun as they returned to Steephank but, as they passed through a copse of hazel bushes, a single ray of sunshine broke through and shone on just one of the saplings. Marguerite had often come this way but had never before noticed *this* stem, now lit brilliantly against the gloom of the leaves under the overcast sky. It had a bine of honeysuckle twisting around it, which in growing had strangled the sapling, forcing it to grow into a curious spiral of tortured wood.

Then, as suddenly as it had appeared, the ray of light

died and the twisted stem became as inconspicuous as before.

She ran on to catch up with Rowan.

Chapter 13

Bluebell was having a bad morning. Not a single salted nut had come her way and she was feeling desperate; she could not get the taste from her mouth. It was there, but it wasn't, and it had to be. She had tried every trick she knew to entertain the Visitors but none of the special nuts was thrown to her. Maybe she could find some around by the bins. It was a forlorn hope as there had never been any there before, scraps of food, yes, but nuts, no, but she still went to look, feeling awful. Her limbs were stiff and her mouth was dry and uncomfortable.

There were Greys talking behind one of the tall metal dustbins. She listened to hear who it was, ready to leave quickly if they were any of the ones who plagued her.

But then, there might be a nut for her. "Salt, salt, salt. Oh, dear Sun, I need that salt." She stayed.

It was a stranger's voice that she heard. "New orders from the Great Lord Silver. Get rid of *all* the Brown Jobs, kill them if need be. We need more Leaping-room. Do whatever you have to. There will be big territories for the most active."

"No constraints?"

Bluebell recognised Quartz's voice.

"None. Do whatever you have to!"

"Right," said Quartz. "We'll soon sort out that decrepit bunch of savages across the pool. I fancy that precinct. We'll get them before sundown. I'm looking forward to this. Yes, sir. Thank you, Stranger."

Thoughts whirled in Bluebell's head. It was Juniper and all her old friends they were talking of killing – that evening!

Her mind cleared suddenly. What a fool she'd been, consorting with these ruthless creatures all this time, just for those nuts. No, she mustn't even think of those; her duty was to warn the others.

Learning of danger
Leap, scramble, climb, hop or run,
Warn all the others.

She turned to go. She would cut through Deepend and reach Steepbank that way. Her claws scratched on the concrete as she moved.

"Quiet." It was Quartz's voice. "Who's there?"

Bluebell froze.

A whispered voice. "You go round that way, I'll take this side."

Bluebell leapt for the top of the bin, her claws scrabbling on the smooth metal lid, and from there to the wood-shingled roof.

"It's the Red – 'Bell. She must have heard the plan – after her!"

Bluebell raced up the grey shingles, her claws biting into the soft cedarwood. She ran over the ridge, jumped across a gap into a tree and scrambled along a branch in the direction of Deepend. She felt dizzy, unused now to climbing and running and, badly out of condition, missed a hold and fell. The Greys behind her were catching up, calling to others on the ground to head her off. Deepend seemed full of Greys, but maybe she could make it around Beachend. She must warn Juniper, her Juniper, she must, she must. The Greys ran too. Stronger, bigger, fitter, they cornered her on the shore below the Man-dreys.

"Sneaks and eavesdroppers don't deserve to die quickly," said Quartz. "Death by nipping, I think. Me first."

Bluebell closed her eyes as she felt his sharp teeth pierce the skin of her left thigh. Then her tail – excruciatingly painful – her ears, forepaws, her nose, her tail again, her back. Her head swam with the pain, the colour faded out of the sky, her legs no longer supported her and she slumped to the ground, kicked spasmodically and then was still. Blood oozed from her nose and dripped on to the sand of the narrow beach.

"That's one for a start," said Quartz as the Greys trooped excitedly up the bank. "More will join her by tonight."

Juniper had watched all this from the opposite side of the pool. He knew that the Red he had seen being chased and attacked must be Bluebell and that it was her limp body on the shore.

They had killed her, killed his Bluebell and just left her there. He burned with anger. Who *were* these squirrels who could do this just so as they could take over the area for themselves? He set off around the head of the pool, through

Deepend, to get to Bluebell. The woods there were teeming with Greys, so he tried to go round by way of Beachend. More Greys; he turned back again along the shore below Steepbank.

Looking to where Bluebell lay in the sun across the pool, he stopped and listened.

"Juniper, Juniper."

A faint voice was calling, some freak of nature carrying the sound along the surface of the water. "Juniper."

Bluebell wasn't dead; she was calling him. His Bluebell – still alive and needing him.

He was frantic. He ran up and down the shoreline. There was no way he could get to her. No way.

But there *was* a way, he realised, and it terrified him. He would have to *swim*.

"Juniper, *Juniper*." Bluebell's voice came again.

Juniper looked at the expanse of water between him and the tiny body. He dared not swim. Memories of being in the water when he had been chased by the Greys overwhelmed him, and he cowered on the beach shivering with fear.

The calls came again: "Juniper, *Juniper*."

He stood up, shook himself, waded into the pool, cold in the shadow of the Steepbank trees, and set off to swim across. He felt the change in the temperature as he swam from the shade into the sunlight, finding it easier in the warmer water. He kept on, guided by Bluebell's calls. "Juniper, *Juniper*, come to me." His bedraggled tail, as thin as a rat's, acted as a rudder, steering him towards her voice.

Then, feeling the coarse sand below his feet, he crawled out, shook off some of the water, waved his tail in an attempt to fluff it and went to where Bluebell lay. Flies rose lazily from her wounds as he approached.

Juniper licked her face and she opened her eyes.

"You came," she said and the lids dropped again.

Juniper waved his tail over her, the sun drying his fur rapidly. He was not sure what to do next. At least he could keep the flies off.

Bluebell opened her eyes again. "The Greys are going to attack Steepbank. This evening. You must warn the . . ." The sentence was never finished. Her tail twitched convulsively. Bluebell the Scavenger had gone Sunwards.

"Well, look at this, then, here's another one. Where did he come from? He must have crept through the pickets." A Grey was looking down from the top of the small bank. "Come on, we'll give *him* the treatment. Down here. Come on."

Juniper turned back to Bluebell but knew it was useless. She was Sun-gone now for sure. He put his paw on her shoulder, looked upwards and said the Farewell Kernel.

> *Sun, take this squirrel*
> *Into the peace of your earth*
> *To nourish a tree.*

The Greys were streaming down the bank. Quickly, without thinking, he entered the water again.

Chapter 14

Rowan and Marguerite returned from the Clay-Pan to find the community in a state of alarm. Juniper's news had spread rapidly and all the squirrels were converging on the Council Tree for an emergency meeting. Oak and Burdock were trying to calm them, but it was apparent to all that the period of indecision must now be over.

When they were all assembled, Oak addressed them.

"My friends, we have lived here together under the Sun for longer than even Old Burdock can remember, and I had hoped to spend the whole of my life in this most beautiful of places, and be able to pass on our traditions to generations yet to be given life. Now, though, the Silver Tide has come, and threatens our very existence. Bluebell Who Sold . . ." He paused. "Bluebell is Sun-gone after an assault by these savage creatures but not before warning us, through Juniper, that they intend to attack us all this evening. None of us knows how to fight and the Greys are bigger and stronger than we are; they also have the Stone force and we have no counter to that.

"It is clear that we must, however reluctantly, give up our Guardianships here and move away to a safer place, if only for the sake of our youngsters."

The squirrels nodded in agreement, but said nothing.

"So," Oak continued, "we must now decide just where. Does anyone have any idea where we might go?"

Again there was silence, each looking at the others for inspiration.

Eventually Chestnut said, "I don't suppose anywhere is safe. Anywhere *we* can go, the Greys can follow, but since they came from the east, clearly we must go westwards."

Rowan said, "If we go west there is a pool with an Eyeland in it. If we could get on to that we would be safe."

"What's an Eyeland?" asked Larch, who had missed hearing Rowan telling of his climbabout adventures.

He described the Eyeland; the perfect proportions of the trees and the pink and white water-flowers, making it all sound so attractive that several wanted to start out for it at once.

"Wait, steady everyone," said Oak. "How big is this Eyeland, Rowan?"

Rowan told him.

"It's a fine idea, but there are 'lots' of us, far too many to live on an Eyeland of that size, even if we could get across the water to it." He looked around forlornly, reluctant to let the idea go. "Does any squirrel know of a bigger Eyeland?"

"Yes," said Heather Treetops, and the other squirrels turned to look at her, for she seldom spoke at meetings. "Sometimes, when I wanted to be alone, and before the Greys came, I would go up to the top of a private Look-out Tree on the other side of our Deepend Guardianship. From there, far away to the east, I could see a huge pool with these 'Eyeland' things in it. Big ones," she added.

"You never told me," said her life-mate, Chestnut.

"Didn't I?" Heather responded innocently.

"How far away?" asked Oak.

"Must be several days' journeying," said Heather, remembering her time on climbabout a few years before.

"Were there trees on these Eyelands?" asked Larch the Curious.

"Covered in them, lots!" said Heather.

"That's the place to go, then," said Oak, thankful for a positive suggestion, then, thinking of the difficulties, added, "assuming we can get there, that is."

They discussed the practicalities. First they would have to go through an area probably now held by Greys, then find a way to cross the water to reach safety on one of the Eyelands.

They all agreed to risk the first danger but no squirrel had a suggestion for the crossing. Finally Old Burdock quoted a Kernel which had not been called on for many generations in their community.

Exiles in danger
Trust in the Sun. Help will come
When least expected.

"We must trust in the Sun," she said, and plans were made to hide from the Greys near the Little Pool that evening and leave the area finally at first light.

Then Burdock said, "Before we go to prepare, I have another subject to discuss. Juniper, will you leave us, please?"

Juniper looked up. A squirrel was only asked to leave a Council Meeting by the Tagger when a tag change was being discussed. Surely he hadn't done anything wrong now? Tail low, he left and waited out of ear-twitch of the Council.

Burdock then said, "I know it is not a custom to give new tags to squirrels after they are Sun-gone but in the case of Bluebell, she gave her life trying to warn us. This was a 'noble' act." Burdock realised that she had used an archaic word from the days when Leaders were born to the job and not "selected" as now, but on glancing round could see that every squirrel understood her meaning. Even Heather Treetops was nodding agreement.

"I don't think we should remember her as Bluebell Who Sold Herself for Peanuts. I am proposing a new tag – Bluebell Who Gave All to Save Us. Any objections?" Burdock looked around. There were no objections, just a murmur of approval.

"Now, Juniper – the Scavenger. For some time this tag has been inappropriate and I have been watching for some action on which to base a new, truer tag. Today, as we know, it happened. Juniper swam the pool to get to Bluebell and then swam back to warn us. Both of these were worthy deeds and I propose that he is now tagged – the Swimmer. To a stranger this may not mean much, but to those of us who recognise his good qualities it will mean a great deal. Any objections?" Once again there were none.

When Juniper was called back and told of his new tag, he was delighted and his tail rose for the first time in moons, mitigating to some extent his sorrow over the loss of Bluebell.

The Reds busied themselves with preparations to leave,

before they all assembled near the Little Pool. Old Burdock suggested to Oak that a whole series of confusing scent-trails be laid and squirrels ran from tree to tree and off along the paths in various directions.

Guards were posted to watch for any Greys, but all the mature squirrels were aware that they had no real plans for defence, and waited apprehensively as the light faded.

Marguerite, observing the preparation of what were clearly inadequate defence plans, thought that it was important to know exactly how many squirrels there were. She counted, reached eight and then stopped. "Lots" came next and that was much too vague. She tried again and still reached "lots".

She counted each family separately. There was her own, consisting of Old Burdock, her grandmother; Oak and Fern, her parents; Rowan, her elder brother and herself. That was five.

Then the Deependers, Heather and Chestnut with their two youngsters, one of whom, Tamarisk, was growing out of the dreyling stage, but was very immature in the way he behaved.

She looked round for the Beachenders and saw them in the next tree. Clover was with her daughter Tansy, and her son. She could not see Larch the Curious, he must be one of the guards. Marguerite counted these on her claws – four more.

Then there was Juniper, he must be on guard duty too.

She tried to work out how many that made altogether. Five and four and four and one. It was "lots" once again!

Tom, the caretaker, was on his rounds with the litter-bag.

He was much later than usual; the sun had been so hot earlier that he had slept most of the afternoon and now had to make up for the time he had lost. He walked along, pausing occasionally to transfer the sweet papers and cigarette packets from the end of his spiked stick to his bag, grumbling to himself and cursing the thoughtlessness of people who just threw their rubbish down anywhere.

Seeing the body of a red squirrel on the beach near the steps, he picked it up by the tail, wrinkled his nose as the flies rose in a cloud, put it in a rabbit-scrape at the foot of a pine tree, covered it over with soil and pressed it down with his foot.

Don't want to upset the visitors, he thought.

At the deep end of the pool he surprised a large party of grey squirrels hopping along the path towards the steep-banked side. There was a kind of menace in the way they were moving. He waved his stick at them and shouted, "Get off with you, you nasty little beggars!"

The squirrels scattered and ran back past the Mandreys.

With dusk closing in, he was collecting the last few pieces of paper on the path above the beach when he again saw the phalanx of Greys heading for the steep-banked side and chased and scattered them once more.

"What in hell are you lot up to?" he shouted.

Chapter 15

The Reds had spent a sleepless night in the trees near the Little Pool waiting for an attack that never came. Now, they were ready to move off even before the sun was over the horizon. They were tense and chattered nervously among themselves in small family groups.

Oak, though, was calmer now. Although unhappy about abandoning the Guardianship which had meant so much to him, sad at leaving the lovely pool and concerned about the hazards of the journey ahead, a decision had been made and he could at last lead them in some action.

Indecision kills.
Act positively and lead.
Action is the Key.

"Right," he said clearly. "If the Greys *are* planning to attack us and find we have gone, they will expect us to head west and follow. So we will start off by going that way and when we pass the Clay-Pan we will turn south, then go east and cross the Great Heath towards the Huge Pool and safety on the Eyelands. No turning back, eyes forward. We leave *now*."

He leapt into the next tree, the others following in an undignified scramble which disentangled after a few trees were passed, until there was an orderly column of squirrels running and leaping in single file through the branches. Fern, preoccupied with grooming her tail, was the last to leave.

Old Burdock leapt with the others but her joints ached and she soon fell back to the last position, behind even Fern, to be joined there by Clover the Carer, who asked if she was all right.

"You may have to leave me behind, Clover-Friend," she panted. "I'll catch up with you later."

Clover ran after the leaders, passing squirrel after squirrel until she was just behind Oak. "Slow down!" she called. "Some of us can't keep up at this pace."

Oak stopped and waited until all the squirrels were together again, then, aware of the differences in ages and fitness within the group, he led off more slowly, looking back frequently for signs of pursuit. Their speed was slowed by Old Burdock who often had to stop for breath and insisted each time that they leave her behind, "to catch up later".

Oak would hear none of this and, by the time they reached the Clay-Pan, the sun was high in the sky and the heat was getting unbearable. All was quiet behind them, and as Old Burdock looked worn out, Oak ordered a halt. They all climbed into the shady branches of the ancient fir overhanging the Clay-Pan to rest, each busy with their thoughts.

Chestnut was having doubts about the wisdom of leaving the area they knew for the unknown. "Are we doing the right thing?" he asked Heather.

"We had no choice," she reminded him. "I hate the idea of just clearing out and leaving my ancestral home to the Greys, but we can survive – and prosper. We'll get to one of those Eyelands and we'll all be safe there. We can start a new life for the youngsters then."

"I hope you're right. I must admit I have my doubts."

Larch, further down the sloping trunk with Clover and their youngster Tansy, was more cheerful. "This is like being on climbabout again, only with company. I'm dying to know what those Eyelands are like. Do you think they will have any pools on them?"

Clover's mind was on other things. She was watching Old Burdock who was dozing fitfully near her.

Larch said, "Do you?"

"Hush, Larch-Pa," said Tansy, indicating Old Burdock with her paw. Larch nodded and shut his eyes.

Oak was worried. The responsibility for the group's safety lay heavy on his shoulders. If they were to survive and reach the Eyelands it was going to be up to him to lead them through unknown country and he had never even been on climbabout. Was he really fit to be Leader? He shook himself.

> *When the cones are down,*
> *Even if you doubt yourself,*
> *Hide all your concerns.*

That was a Kernel the Tagger taught to newly elected

Leaders. It was important not to let fear show. Make decisions – lead! Even if the decision should subsequently be proved wrong, action could then be taken to correct and recover. *Action* was the *Key*.

Should he be doing something positive now? More doubts assailed him, but he only had to look at Old Burdock slumped across the branch below to know that if he wanted her wisdom for the journey and on the Eyeland, they must wait until she was fit to travel again.

Fern was unconcernedly grooming herself on a nearby branch.

Marguerite and Rowan were together, looking down at her numbers, still visible where she had scratched them in the clay surface the day before. "There's the eight that you drew." She pointed it out to him.

A pair of lizards ran across the hot dry clay. Rowan wanted to chase them.

Juniper had climbed to the very highest part of the tree and was looking back at where he knew the Blue Pool lay sparkling in the sun. Farewell, Bluebell-Mate, he was thinking, I wish I had been able to bury you under a tree, but at least you are free of the grey monsters now. He came down slowly and settled on the trunk where there was a patch of shade. He yawned and closed his eyes. Oak would wake him when it was time to go.

Just after High Sun Oak woke up from a doze and looked down. "Lots" of Greys were fanning out across the dry white clay below, following the footprints and the scents left by his party.

Rowan was also awake. He glanced at Oak, then slipped

down the upper side of the trunk, ran along the top of the bank, showed himself on the skyline and shouted.

"Flea-ridden tree-rats," he called. "Sun-damn you all!" and he disappeared into the heather and bracken, heading westwards.

The Reds, all awake but silent in the leaning tree above, watched the posse of Greys chase after Rowan as he ran along the bank and off into the heather. The squirrel-chatter faded into the distance.

Oak turned to Fern. "A son to be proud of," he said, his tail high.

Rowan raced on along the dusty heath path, the sun beating down on him. At a crossways he ran a little way along each track, then leapt over a clump of heather to confuse and delay the Greys. He could hear them behind him now and ran faster, leading them away from the vulnerable group in the tree above the Clay-Pan. Then suddenly he felt an inexplicable urge to turn aside and stop. Something, a sensation in the base of his whiskers, had said, "Turn and stop here."

He hopped sideways off the path, knocking over the base part of a broken bottle as he did so, and crouched down to wait.

The Greys had paused at the crossways and were arguing amongst themselves, some saying the Brown Job had gone one way and some another. Then he heard an urgent, confident shout. "This way, this way."

Rowan crouched lower, convinced that his hiding place had been found out, then, smelling the terrifying scent of smoke, he turned his head and saw how the rays of the sun were being focused by the bottle-base on to a wisp of dry moss in which a tiny flame was already showing. He crawled backwards away from the miniature fire. The flame grew, caught the bone-dry heather and suddenly and explosively leapt from clump to clump, fanned by a westerly breeze which seemed to have come from nowhere.

The fire, spreading ever wider, swept down on the Greys and he could hear their shrieks and screams as it overwhelmed them. Then there was just the crackling of the burning heather stems.

Rowan waited upwind of the flames, then, as they moved away over the ridge between him and the Clay-Pan, he tried to follow the fire back the way he had come. In his haste he burned his paws badly and, despite repeated attempts, was unable to walk more than a few steps until the following morning.

At the first scent of burning heather on the breeze, Oak had scrambled to the highest branch of the fir. He could see the billowing smoke-clouds, lit from underneath by the red and orange flames, coming downwind towards them on an ever widening front. Coming too fast to race away from, particularly with Old Burdock unable to move quickly. There was a chance that if they stayed in the tree the flames might not reach them, but he had once seen a burning tree and was not going to risk that. There was only one other option.

He called down, "Every squirrel. Drop out of the tree and crouch in the centre of the Clay-Pan. The fire can't reach us there. It has to feed on plants!" Squirrels fell from the tree like rain and huddled together on the dry clay beneath it as the fire roared past, small pines and birches flaring up as their needles and leaves scorched, shrivelled and burnt. The leaning tree above them, although enveloped in smoke, escaped the flames and gave some protection from the hot embers falling out of the smoke-clouds.

They crouched there for what seemed hours, coughing the smoke out of their lungs, until the air cleared enough for them to look around. They felt very vulnerable in the open, but they had nowhere else to go until the ground cooled. There was no sign of Rowan or the Greys; they must all have died in the fire. But these were unspoken thoughts.

Oak kept testing the ground on the eastern side of the Clay-Pan until, just before dusk, he judged it cool enough for them to cross. Even so there were some scorched paws before they were through the burnt area. They returned part of the way they had come and were relieved to find that the fire had passed to the south of the Little Pool and missed the Blue Pool altogether, but Oak would not let them venture too near. That morning's posse had contained only a small number of the Greys, and others might be waiting for them.

They passed over an area of open heath dotted with small pines and birches but none within leaping distance of the others, and so the whole party had to stay together on the ground, fearful of being caught in the open by a fox. They need not have worried; the resident foxes had slipped away at the first scent of smoke.

The squirrels passed clumps of gorse, dark and menacing in the fading light, and, in the small boggy places where marsh gentians flowered, they cooled their paws on the damp moss.

It was when they came to the two metal lines across their route that Oak finally called a halt. These needed careful examination. He was not going to risk crossing whatever these were, in the dark.

They climbed a tree and tried to sleep, Marguerite finding sleep especially evasive as she grieved for her lost brother.

Rowan had spent a sleepless, painful night in the open. In the morning, soaked by a shower of rain which also put out the last remnants of the fire, he found he was able to hobble back to the Clay-Pan, passing the burnt bodies of the Greys on the way. Except for the leaning tree, everything there was scorched and black, and, finding no sign of his companions in the tree and all scent obliterated by the overwhelming smell of the damp burned foliage, he searched for their bodies, feeling sick with the horror of it all. It was hopeless; too vast an expanse. Hopeless, hopeless. His paws throbbed with pain.

Somewhere out there must be the charred remains of his family and friends, but he might search for days and then never find them.

He thought of his water-flower pool with the dream Eyeland and turned sadly away westwards, alone.

A skylark sang incongruously above the blackened heathland and in the distance a curlew circled over the site of its nest, mournfully bubbling its loss.

Chapter 16

After the shower had passed, Oak looked at the railway lines in the grey dawn light, unable to comprehend their purpose, then, seeing how they continued into the distance to either side of them, touched one cautiously. It seemed harmless enough, so he clambered over one slippery rail and then the other, before encouraging the others to follow him. The youngsters and elderly squirrels were helped over and the party of exiles went on along the side of a field, hearing dogs barking from a Man-drey, but too far away to inflict hound-dread on even the most nervous. Then through a hedge, down into a ditch, up the other side and they came to a roadway, smelling of oil and rubber, familiar to them from the car park at Humanside.

There was no traffic to be seen in the early light and they crossed in single file, wriggling under a gate on the far side into another field with a wood to their right, behind an earthen bank riddled with rabbit holes. The rabbits, nibbling their last mouthfuls before lying up for the day, ignored the squirrels who passed them silently through the cool dewy grass.

The group were moving more slowly now, resting

frequently for the sake of Old Burdock and those with sore paws, convinced that there was now no immediate pursuit and intent only on getting to the Huge Pool and finding, with the Sun's help, some way to cross to the Eyelands and safety.

By evening, after a long rest in a lone pine tree at High Sun, they had reached a stream with willow and alder trees on either side. In the hollow they lost sight of the familiar outline of Screech Hill behind them, and a small wood hid the view ahead. Oak and Juniper climbed a tree to plan a route, the others keeping watch below. They could see the Huge Pool in the distance and how the stream widened into a series of marshy pools with spear-grass growing around the edges.

A woodpecker, glowing green and yellow in the light of the setting sun, flew in to land on its favourite rotten alder, saw the squirrels and turned away, rising and falling through the air with its strange undulating flight. It seemed to be laughing at them in a high-pitched human voice.

In the swamp below were unfamiliar rushes with brown furry flowers which reminded Oak of the tail of the cat that had once lived around the Man-dreys at the Blue Pool. A wave of homesickness hit him and he turned to look back, but there was nothing to see but the grass-covered rise in the ground and grazing cows on the skyline.

> *If it hurts too much*
> *Thinking of what cannot be,*
> *Put it out of mind.*

He shook his head violently, turned to Juniper and said,

"We'll follow the edge of the swamp, keeping near the trees so that we can retreat into them if we need to. I'd like to go through the treetops, but Old Burdock can't leap for long and the gaps are too wide for some of the youngsters."

Cows looked up briefly from their grazing as the group passed, some of the squirrels pausing to eat the ripe blackberries and the hips and haws in the bushes around them. Sloes, black, but with a dusty bloom on the drupes, covered the twigs of blackthorn bushes, but the Reds, knowing the dryness these gave in the mouth, ignored them and hurried on. When it was nearly dark, Oak called a halt and they all climbed a friendly alder tree to huddle together in the darkness.

Each night was becoming a little colder than the last and there was a tang of autumn in the air at dawn. One morning there was another scent as well, one that Juniper recognised as salt, and he had to fight to keep the old craving from overwhelming him. He remembered his Bluebell and was determined not to let it dominate him again.

The squirrels fed uneasily on the plentiful food all about them. They saw where bark had been stripped off a number of young trees and there were cones lying about under a pine tree which bore the marks of larger teeth than theirs. The distinctive scent of Greys was there too. It was only an elusive hint in the air, but to those who had lived in close proximity to them for a while there was also something else, more sensed by whiskers than by nose, ear, or eye. A sense of arrogance, contempt almost, possession by right of might.

The Reds looked about them, feeling that this must be a

part of some Greys' territory, then scrambled through the scrubby trees, alert for danger, until they reached a shoreline of muddy banks with clumps of rushes. Water lapped on to the beach. Burdock went forward and tasted it.

"This isn't a pool!" she said. "This is the sea.

Pools have sweet water.
Bitter water makes the sea,
You can't get round it.

"That's a Kernel for squirrels going on climbabout. I never thought I would see it, though. We have come to the *sea*."

"Now what do we do?" asked Chestnut, looking out to where the tree-covered Eyelands appeared to float on the rippling water.

"Trust in the Sun," said Burdock, after a pause. "We've got this far safely." Then, lowering her voice, added, "Apart from Rowan, that is."

The squirrels spread out along the shoreline, where the water jostled twigs and pieces of broken reed-stem at the very highest tide mark.

"I think the sea is going away!" said Marguerite a few minutes later. "Look, this stone was under the water when I came past it, and now the top of it is sticking out."

The squirrels gathered round and watched. Eventually even Chestnut the Doubter was convinced that the sea was indeed going away and soon they would be able to walk across to the nearest Eyeland. Marguerite realised that if they could, then the Eyelands would not be safe havens for them. She spoke her fears quietly to Burdock. "Trust in the

Sun," she was told and had to be content with that, as they watched the sea continue to slide away over the mud-flats towards the Eyelands.

They sat in the short grass along the shoreline, fascinated by the disappearing sea, until High Sun, most of them hoping that a dry path would appear to enable them to cross to the Eyelands. Even Oak forgot the possibility of danger from landwards, until Heather, who had looked over her shoulder, whispered to him, "Don't move suddenly, Oak-Friend, but there's a posse of Greys behind us."

Oak turned his head casually as though looking at the sky to judge the time, and saw the Greys, lots and lots, all watching them ominously.

"No squirrel turn around," he said calmly. "Just start walking towards the Eyelands where the sea has been. *Don't* look back."

The Reds did as they were told and walked out on to the slowly drying mudbanks, which got stickier and stickier under their paws as they neared the water.

Fern the Fussy stopped to lick some of the foul-tasting mire off her tail and saw the Greys following them menacingly, although keeping some distance behind. With their greater weight they were sinking further into the mud than the Reds.

Ahead, the sea appeared to have stopped going away and the fugitives waited there uncertainly, sinking in the cloying ooze at the water's edge.

The Greys, also picking their way carefully, were still trying to advance, but without their usual cockiness, their fur becoming covered in a grey slime until they also halted some yards back and stared silently at the Reds on the mudbank below them.

For several minutes both sides crouched, neither moving, the Greys apparently waiting for something to happen.

"The sea is coming back," wailed Tamarisk, "it's all over my feet."

The Greys laughed and nudged one another. "Time and tide wait for no squirrel," one of them called out and the others all laughed again.

The sun shone down from a cloudless sky on to the red and the grey squirrels, the heat drying the slime on their fur. It also shone on a discarded door floating along on the rising tide beyond the trapped Reds, touching the shore from time to time, then lifting and drifting on as the tide inexorably rose higher. The Leader of the Greys saw it coming and started to move forward but was unable to do so without sinking dangerously into the mud.

Oak, seeing the Greys watching something behind him, turned, saw the door himself and recognised that here was a chance of escape.

"Follow me," he shouted, leaping for the door as it touched against the mudbank, and the others leapt after him, although Old Burdock, spluttering and spitting salty water, had to be unceremoniously hauled aboard. The door, pushed from the shore by the impact of the leaping bodies, drifted away, turning slowly as it did so.

Tamarisk the Tactless, feeling safe now, put his paw to his nose and wiggled his claws at the frustrated Greys, who were retreating in disorder. The Reds did not see the fate of the Greys as the door, its surface now awash with water, drifted around a mud-spit, and caught an offshore breeze. Each squirrel had to dig its claws into the soft wood and cling on for dear life.

Chapter 17

———

"The Eyelands are going away," Burdock reported to Oak as they drifted along. The squirrels were getting used to the strange way the door moved on the water; some had even started to scramble about, their bodies adjusting to the movement as they did in wind-tossed treetops. All were wet from the wavelets that sloshed over the door from time to time, but the sun was warm and none was seriously chilled. Unfamiliar long-necked black birds flew heavily past and gulls, normally seen only rarely by the squirrels when storms forced seabirds inland, were everywhere, looking down with cold yellow eyes on the door and its unusual passengers, and squawking their disapproval.

Marguerite the Bright One was oblivious to all of this and to the rocking motion under her feet. Painted on the wood where she sat was one of *her* numbers and one she didn't know. There was a 4 and then a number with no corners in it at all – 0. What could this last number mean? No corners meant that there was nothing to record. A number for nothing? That did not make any kind of sense. She scratched at the figures as if this would make them reveal their true meaning, but the flaking paint came off

OURLAND
BROWNSEA ÍSLAND

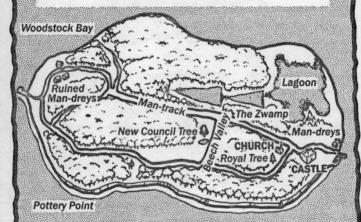

Woodstock Bay

Ruined Man-dreys

Man-track

New Council Tree

Beech Valley

Lagoon

The Zwamp

Man-dreys

CHURCH
Royal Tree

CASTLE

Pottery Point

Furzey Island

under her claws, broke up and floated away on the next wave to wash over their raft.

Old Burdock was repeating to herself, "Trust in the Sun. Trust in the Sun." Marguerite joined her and soon all the squirrels were chanting in unison.

Oak stood precariously, swaying with the motion under his feet. "The Eyelands are coming back," he said and the chanting stopped as every squirrel turned and looked in the direction he was pointing. They all agreed that the Eyelands were indeed getting nearer as they watched, the door drifting in towards the shore of the largest.

Finally, to the huge relief of every squirrel, the door grounded and, glad to be on land again, they were able to walk ashore over wet but firm, gravelly sand, from which strange half-buried round and rectangular objects projected. They clustered together amongst the flotsam at the top of the beach.

It was Larch the Curious who made the first move. "Come on," he said, "let's go look and see what there is to see."

"But we don't know where we are," replied Chestnut.

"We never will if we stay here!" Heather pointed out.

Oak, though still feeling slightly queasy from the unaccustomed movement of the door, felt it was time to assert himself.

Firm Leadership shown
Provides other squirrels with
A common purpose.

"We will go carefully, all staying together. No squirrel is

107

to go off on their own. We don't know what dangers might be lurking here."

The beach and the foreshore where they had come aground were littered with broken drainage pipes and misfired bricks, the debris from a pottery which had once occupied the site. Broken shards were everywhere, many overgrown with herbage, and even the large pines behind the foreshore grew out of mounds and banks of soil covering old scrap heaps. The whole area had an unreal and disturbing sense for the tired animals.

Tansy looked unhappy and whimpered, "I don't like it here, let's go home."

Clover went over to her and said, "The Sun has guided and helped us to get here, I don't think we *can* go home. Don't forget those Greys are there now."

The mention of the Greys made all the other squirrels look around but there was no sense of danger even after the most vigorous sniffing and whisker-twitching. Certainly there was no scent of fox or grey squirrel although Juniper and Oak thought they could detect just a whiff of strange Reds. However, with the breeze blowing from behind them and the salt smell from the sea, neither could be sure.

Tamarisk the Tactless was snuffling at an old crab shell on the beach. "This place stinks," he pronounced loudly.

Keeping together, they climbed the bank of soil-covered, broken pipes to the grass under the pines and sensed the air again. Now there was nothing but a benign and even slothful feeling, not the slightest hint of danger of any kind.

The squirrels spread out a little and, staying on the ground, made their way through the coarse grass and bracken to the top of the next bank. There was still no sign of any animals other than harmless rabbits and, with the sun setting behind them, they prepared for their first night in the safety of an Eyeland. Food was everywhere. The squirrels ate well and started to relax in the peaceful atmosphere, later sleeping in family groups in the upper branches of a large pine.

"We will explore in the morning," Oak told them.

There seemed to be no reason to hurry when the sun first showed itself through the trees to the east, and after an especially thankful morning prayer the party foraged in a leisurely way, before moving further inland in a loose group on the ground, to find out exactly what the Eyeland had in store for them. Passing through clumps of rhododendrons and crossing several overgrown Man-paths, they came to a place where these tracks passed below some magnificent mature pines, their high branches forming a canopy over a light brown carpet of fallen needles. Above they could hear squirrel sounds. The exiles crowded together and waited expectantly.

Red squirrels came down the trees and stared at them. None spoke, and Oak, knowing that *they* were the strangers, signalled to his party to keep their tails low.

The Eyeland squirrels circled the newcomers suspiciously, led by an elderly and dignified Red who kept his tail high.

"Who are yew, and from whence have yew come?" he asked.

"Who are these funny foreigners?" Marguerite whispered to Burdock.

"Shush. We are the foreigners here. Keep your tail down," replied Burdock.

No lands are Foreign
It is those who pass through that
Are the foreigners.

Oak replied, "I am Oak the Cautious, Leader of this party, and this is Burdock the Tagger, this is Fern the Fussy – my life-mate, this is . . ." He introduced each member of the exiles in turn, down to and including every tagged youngster, as is proper. Each raised and lowered his tail in the traditional manner. "We have come from the Blue Pool." He could explain more later. Then, remembering the tradition, he added, "We greet you . . ." and paused, not yet knowing the name and tag of the Leader.

The distinguished-looking squirrel stepped forward and bowed to Fern, who looked sideways at Oak and fluffed her tail proudly, hoping that there were no tangles visible.

"Uz iz King Willow the Third, zon of King Azpen the Fourth, zon of King Cyprezz the Won and Only, zon of King Willow the Zecond, zon of King Poplar the Fifth, zon of . . ." The Leader went on and on through a poll-list of ancestors, his tail high with evident pride, then turned to a female at his side and introduced her.

"This is Kingz-Mate Thizle the Zecond, daughter of Rozebay, daughter of Cowzlip, daughter of Groundzel, daughter of . . ." This list, too, seemed to go on for ever.

Burdock listened with interest. The naming pattern was the same as her community used, tree-names for males, flower-names for females, but the tags, if one could call them that, told one nothing about their characters, and after one generation or, at the most two, parentage gave no guide as to what to expect from *that* individual.

King Willow then turned to one of the younger squirrels. "And thiz iz my zon, Next-King Zallow." He indicated a narrow-chested squirrel with a slight squint.

The exiles braced themselves for another string of names and sighed audibly when he passed straight on, introducing another, more handsome son, Poplar, and a nephew, Fir. Then a daughter, Teazle, and lastly two nieces, Voxglove and Cowzlip, who together would have weighed as much as one healthy squirrel.

The half-dozen or so other squirrels who sat with lowered tails he did not introduce, but with a wave of his paw said, "And theze are zome of the zervantz."

"What is the name of this land?" Oak asked, when he realised that the formal greeting was not being returned.

'Thiz iz *Ourland*," replied King Willow. Then, seeming to lose his suspicion, he and each of his family passed along the line of exiles, brushing their whiskers with their own, in a special and rather pleasant form of greeting. The exiles felt free to raise their tails and relax, mixing with the Ourlanders and making friends, the youngsters from each party romping and playing together in the pine trees and running wildly about in the grassy glades.

Oak, cautious as usual, asked King Willow if they should not go up into a tree for safety and was asked why.

"To be safe from surprise by a fox or a dog."

"What is voxez and dogz?" asked King Willow. "There'z nothing here to harm uz."

Burdock was talking to Kingz-Mate Thizle, asking about Ourland.

"There iz water all round it, no other zquirrelz can come here, and that huz been our problem. There'z no choize of maytz now. Brotherz have to mate with their zizterz or cloze couzinz, even if it feelz the wrong thing to do."

Burdock was appalled. One of the most important Kernels said:

> *Never mate with kin.*
> *Seek new blood for strong dreylings,*
> *They are your future.*

"Why don't they chose mates from other families?" she asked.

Kingz-Mate Thizle looked round sadly. "There aren't any good wonz now. Only the zervantz' familiez, and uz *obviouzly* can't mate with thoze." She wrinkled her nose disparagingly. "Uz are all that are left and uz don't have many dreylingz now. Mozd of the wonz that are born each year are zickly and are Zun-gone afore their firzt winter. Perhapz that'z why the Zun zent all of yew. Welcome to Ourland."

Burdock was pleased that these strange Reds shared their respect for the Sun even if some of their other customs were different. She acknowledged the welcome with a lowering of the head and a sideways flick of her tail.

Chapter 18

Burdock and King Willow were lying out in the upper branches of the Royal Macrocarpa Tree which grew near an abandoned church. From here they could look out over the meadow where the humans obligingly fed the peacocks which strutted about between the Royal Tree and the grounds of Brownsea Castle.

This magnificent multi-trunked tree stood proudly on a high bank, and the resting squirrels could see over the castle to the Poole Harbour entrance and the open sea beyond. They could watch the car ferry as it shuttled back and forth between Sandbanks and South Haven Point, but the squirrels were no more concerned with this than with the sailing boats dotting the harbour, part of a strange Man-world beyond their shores and of no interest to them.

The autumn harvest was in full swing, and so plentiful were nuts of every kind that only a few hours of gathering and hiding each day were sufficient to ensure a well-fed winter. King Willow never gathered nuts. "Let the zervantz do that," he had said, even offering their services to Oak, Fern and Burdock. There were plenty of them to do so, all apparently just there to make life easy for the Royals.

The exiles politely refused, preferring to make their own provision as they had always done.

Save for the future,
Store plentiful nuts safely,
Prepare for lean times.

Somehow it did not seem right to let others do this for them.

The two elderly squirrels often lay out on fine days swapping legends and traditions. Many of the Ourland customs were quite unlike those practised on the mainland and at first Burdock had been appalled to learn that the Sun-tithe, which was such an essential part of their mainland life, had deteriorated here into a mere ritual. Although the Ourland squirrels still stored nuts for the winter days and for the leaner times of early spring, they had forgotten the reason for leaving some undisturbed.

One out of eight nuts
Must be left to germinate.
Here grows our future.

King Willow could not remember the whole of that Kernel. He had mumbled something about "eight nutz being left" and described how each autumn they buried eight nuts together, which were never to be dug up, and then forgot about them until it was time to do the same thing at the next harvest.

"But what about future trees?" Burdock had asked.

"Never zeemed to be a problem," replied King Willow

listlessly. "The deerz eat zum new zeedlingz and the rabbitz eat zum but there alwayz zeem to be enough each year. Maybe it only matterz where yew com'z from."

Burdock was interested in the absence of tagging. With the Ourlanders there seemed to be no sign of any system of reward or punishment. The Ourland Royal youngsters had, at first, appeared to be a spoilt lot, pampered by their parents, but in fact, now that they were maturing, she had grown fond of them. They seemed willing to learn and had joined in with the newcomers when she taught "Kernels, Traditions and Manners", although most of the elder Ourlanders ignored her teaching sessions.

"Have you never had punishments?" she asked King Willow.

"Oh yez, when uz wuz Next-King we had a zquirrel who wuz called The Nipper. He wuz a half-brother of my father the King, zo muzt have been a zort of uncle to me. Pure white he wuz, with funny pink eyz. Nazty fellow him; if zomeone upzet the King he told The Nipper to bite that zquirrel'z whizkerz off. Have yew ever zeen a zquirrel without whizkerz? Totally lozt, yew don't realize how important they are until yew haven't got any. Lozt mine once. Zun, it wuz awful!"

"What had yew – you done?" Burdock asked, fascinated.

"Uz fanzied a female, a couzin of mine, won of my year, but my father, old King Azpen, had hiz eye on her too. Zo he zent The Nipper to teach me a lezzon. No mating for me that year, uz could hardly climb and didn't dare jump until uz'z whizkerz had grown again. Yew juzt feel zick all the time, zort of out of touch with what iz going on around yew."

"What happened then?" asked Burdock, trying to imagine a whiskerless world.

"Old King Azpen went Zunwardz that winter and uz became King, zo uz bit off The Nipper'z whizkerz uzzelf and zent him off to live in the Zwamp. Put him under a taboo. No zquirrel wuz ever to mention him again and he huz not been zeen zinze. Gone Zunwardz himzelf long ago uz exzpectz, good riddanze too. When uz wuz dreylingz uz uzed to zcare one another in the duzk by calling out 'The Nipperz behind yew'." He chuckled. "Zcared uz all rigid, he did! Nazty old fellow.

"Uz got that female too. Her'z Kingz-Mate Thizle now. Zeemed odd mating with won of my father'z fanzy femalz but with zo few of uz now, uz have got uzed to that kind of thing."

Burdock shuddered. Kin-mating was abhorrent, every Kernel she knew in that area spoke against it, yet she understood the dilemma in which the Ourlanders had found themselves. Ultimately the urge to mate would overcome all taboos. No wonder they were glad to greet the newcomers.

"Was that the only punishment?" she asked.

"If any of the zervantz hurt a Royal, he lozt hiz tail. Another of The Nipper'z jobz. He told uz wonz that he wuz really a kind old zoul and knew how much it would hurt if he bit it all off at wonz, zo to make it hurt lezz he would bite off only an inch each day. Uz never knew if he wuz joking."

Old Burdock said nothing, she just looked at the King, sprawled on the branch laughing quietly to himself, then out to sea. Soon she would go and do some more harvesting.

"That granddaughter of yourz – Marguerite," King Willow said, unexpectedly. "In the zpring uz will mate her with Next-King Zallow. Her may not be a Royal but uz can't be too choozey nowadayz. Her iz a chief'z daughter and a good looker too."

Burdock did not know how to reply. They were still regarded, and regarded themselves, as strangers in another's Guardianship, and had accepted that they must try and live by the local rules, but her knowledge of the ancient Kernels still provided the basis for all her decisions.

> Not even parents
> Can choose a squirrel's life-mate.
> The Sun guides self-choice.

This Kernel was clearly applicable here. She would need to think of a way round this which would not antagonise the King. She excused herself and slipped away down the trunk.

Later she spoke to Oak, and told him what King Willow had suggested. He was appalled. "Next-King Zallow is a *squimp*," he said. "Marguerite would never want *him* for a life-mate."

"I'm not sure that that is exactly what was being suggested," Burdock replied. "There was no mention of 'life', but so much is different here I could not be sure. Do we tell Marguerite what is being planned?"

"Oh yes. You tagged her well with 'the Bright One'. I'll tell her what the King said and see what her reaction is. Sometimes I think she's cleverer than all of us."

Chapter 19

Marguerite had other things on her mind. She kept thinking of the painted figures she had seen on the door as they were floating over to Ourland. One was clearly a four, almost exactly as she had invented it, with four corners in it to check against one's claws. But the other number had no corners at all. It had been round like a pebble or a bird's egg. Who would want a number for nothing? A number for nothing, there must be some other meaning. Sitting at the top of the beach she drew her numbers with her claws in the damp sand.

$$1 2 3 4 5 6 7 4 \text{ and then } 0$$

Was "0" the number that came after eight, instead of "lots"?

She glanced Sunwards as though for guidance, then back at her figures. A tiny piece of glass, polished by the sand and waves, was glinting in the centre of the 0, reflecting the sunlight. The answer must be in that 0, she thought, and as she studied the symbols, a seagull, passing overhead, emptied its bowels and the stinking white guano splattered

down on to the line of figures, obliterating most of the 4
and leaving only enough showing to read as a 1.

1, 2, 3, 4, 5, 6, 7, 1 0, she now read, and in a flash the
answer was with her. After seven, there was *one* lot of eight
and NO more.

If there was another it would be 11, one lot of eight and 1
more, then 12, one lot of eight and 2 more. It was so
obvious, but the Sun did have strange ways of enlightening
the Seeking Squirrel! She skipped up and down the beach
joyfully, needing to tell someone. "There *are* numbers after
eight!" she wanted to shout and rushed off to find Old
Burdock, who always had time for her.

In the open ground above the beach she saw her father
hurrying in her direction so she ran to him and breathlessly
started to explain about her discovery.

Oak held up a paw to check her. "Just a minute, just a
minute, Marguerite-Lass, listen to me first. Old Burdock
has just told me that King Willow wants to mate you with
Next-King Sallow in the spring. I thought you should
know," he added lamely, realising as he said it that he had
acted out of character. Spring was a long way off and he
should have spent more time thinking the implications
through, before blurting it out to his beloved daughter.

Marguerite hardly heard him, her mind full of magical
numbers. After one lot of eight and 7 more – 1 7 – would
come 2 0, two lots of eight and NO more, then ... Her
mind raced away: 21, 22 ... 2 7, 30, 31, 32 ... Numbers
could go on for ever!

Oak tried to listen and understand as she described it all
to him. He would have to tell her about King Willow's

plans when she had calmed down and would heed him.

This took some time. Marguerite would spend hours on the beach, trying out numbers in different combinations: 12, 21, 23, 43, 34, 33, 6 7, 66 ... and having finished a session, signed the symbols in the sand with her special mark – X.

Several times Oak and Burdock had told her about King Willow's plan to mate her with Next-King Sallow in the spring but she would only reply, "Him, he's a squimp!" as though this would end the whole matter. Oak and Burdock were not as sure.

An air of estrangement was building up between the two communities. King Willow had expected his proposal for the mating to have been eagerly agreed to, but it was apparent that Marguerite was not, to say the least, overjoyed at the proposal. "Who did her think her wuz?" he remarked one day to Kingz-Mate Thizle. "The whole Sun-damned lot of them huz come unazked to Ourland and iz eating away az though it belongz to them! They'z even burying uz nutz to eat in the zpring and now rejecting uz zon and heir. If only The Nipper wuz alive, he would teach won or two of them a lezzon."

Kingz-Mate Thizle was not really listening. Her mind was full of pictures of healthy young grandchildren leaping around in the branches of the Great Macrocarpa. "Yes, uz'z zure yew iz right," was all she said.

King Willow summoned Oak to come, alone, to a meeting at the Royal Tree.

"Uz have dezided," he said imperiously, "that yew and yewr party are being too free with uz harvezt and taking advantage of uz generozity. In future yew will reztrict yewr-zelvez to the weztern end of *Our*land." He put a heavy emphasis on "Our".

"That iz all," he said, dismissing the stunned Oak with a wave of his paw.

Oak returned, tail low, to summon a Council Meeting of the exiles. He described his session with King Willow.

"He may be King," said Heather. "Even so we should ignore him. He speaks from under his tail. He can't hurt us. There are as many of us as there are of them and, if hop comes to leap, the zervantz would be on our side."

This was probably true. Two of them, a female called Woodlouze and a male, Zpider, were now regularly attending Old Burdock's training sessions, as were the younger Royals with the exception of Next-King Sallow, though it was unlikely that King Willow was aware of this. Some of the other zervantz visited at quiet times to talk with the exiles. Zpider had realised after one such visit that for the first time in his life he was walking with his tail raised. He lowered it quickly before any of the Royals saw him.

"It's not as simple as that," said Burdock. "We are still the foreigners here. Remember how *we* felt when the Greys came and ignored *our* wishes?"

"But all the Kernels are on our side," said Chestnut. "Aren't they?" He looked at Burdock.

"There are no Kernels regarding Royalty," she replied, "only on how chosen Leaders should behave. There are plenty of them and none gives the right to force-mate a female against her wishes."

"I haven't said I won't take Next-King Sallow yet," said Marguerite, and the squirrels looked at her in surprise.

"Let's leave that issue until the spring, and talk about living in the west of Ourland apart from the others until then."

A swaying sapling
Survives the storm. Stubborn trees
Often get blown down.

Chapter 20

It was not a good winter. Although there was plenty of food, the winds blew cold and rain was so frequent that it soaked into the dreys, chilling the squirrels inside.

On rare sunny days they would come out and run around on the ground and through the trees, enjoying the sunshine and the feel of the blood flowing through their veins. Then, resting, they would discuss what was likely to happen in the spring if King Willow insisted on pursuing his plans for a mating of Marguerite with Next-King Sallow. Marguerite seemed the least bothered of them all. "I can handle that squimp," she would say, but Oak and Old Burdock especially were concerned about the consequences for the Westerners if the Royals had cause to take umbrage.

Fern was not so sure that the proposed mating would be a bad thing.

"It would make our Marguerite the next King's-Mate," she said to Oak one evening. "That would be something!"

"I'm going to pretend I didn't hear that," said Oak sternly. "The only one of that bunch worth a nutshell is Poplar, and the King doesn't even seem to notice that he exists. I'd rather she chose Tamarisk than Sallow!"

"Tamarisk the Tactless? She'd never choose him."

"I know that. All I'm saying is that it has to be *her* choice, I'm not having my – our daughter force-mated with any squirrel. Especially Sallow."

Marble was not enjoying that winter either. Alone for most of the time in his drey in the stunted spruce, he had ample time to reflect on his changed circumstances. Hope of power and influence at Woburn was clearly gone for ever. His ambitions of becoming the Great Lord Silver seemed ludicrous to him now.

His lifeline was Gabbro, who hopped over every time news was brought by passing Greys. This happened often as the Silver Tide swept on through the south-west of New America.

"There is a whole new batch resting up on their way through to some place the natives know as the Wall of Corn. Sandy says she is going on with them, and would I let you know? No hard feelings, she said, but these are a vigorous lot and you know how she likes Lustees."

Marble rubbed the stump of his missing paw and looked out of his drey, to where a cold mist swirled past the entrance.

"When are they going?" he asked.

"Today I think, could even be gone by now. There's not much daylight for travelling in winter and they've got a long way to go!"

Marble said nothing but Gabbro noted the forlorn look on his friend's face.

"Seems it's all bad news today," he said. "There are rumours of some kind of illness about. The Lustees did not know much about it, but it's bad down near the Bright Stone area. Hope it doesn't come here!" Gabbro looked out of the drey. "I'd better be off, the mist is thickening up. See you in a few days." He scrambled down through the scratchy dead twigs of the spruce and was gone.

Gradually spring emerged, heralded by the greening of the hawthorn bushes. The squirrels on the island tasted the fresh buds and combed the hazels for pollen-laden catkins, a welcome change from stored nuts. Marguerite was at this pleasant task when Next-King Sallow came courting, finding her sitting in a hazel bush with yellow pollen around her mouth and on her whiskers.

She hardly noticed him. She had been counting as she ate, seven lots of eight and six more, 76. Seven lots of eight and seven more, 77. She stopped. What came next? Since she had been Sun-inspired to abandon the figure 8, she could go no further. Was this as far as numbers could go?

Next-King Sallow called up to her. "Hello, my pretty one."

Marguerite looked down at him. He was pale and his tail was scraggy and thin. "Are you speaking to me?" she asked, peering around as though to see some other squirrel that he might have been addressing.

"Yez. Yew my pretty," he said, her scent floating tantalisingly down to him in the warm spring sunshine.

Marguerite assessed his strength and likely stamina. "If you want me, you'll have to catch me," she called teasingly.

She leapt for the nearest tree. "One," she counted, ran through the branches and leapt into the next. "Two."

At "six lots of eight and seven more", 67, she looked

back and was amazed to find that Sallow was still following. She glimpsed other squirrels watching the chase from trees or from the ground.

Innocently unaware of the mating-scent trailing behind her which was whipping Sallow into a frenzy of un-accustomed activity, she ran and leapt on.

At seven lots of eight and seven more, 77, Marguerite found that either by accident or by Sallow's design she was in a tree on the edge of the wide Man-track with him close behind her. She would have to try a leap greater than she had ever attempted before or submit to Sallow and mate with him, and this was tree number 77.

Was the Sun saying, "There are no more numbers after 77, your destiny *is* to be mated with Sallow?"

She turned, looked into his leering dog-like face, saw the red foam bubbling around his mouth and felt a kind of hound-dread trying to paralyse her body, but, with a massive effort of will, she suppressed the hound-dread, gathered her strength, ran down a branch and leapt into space.

She cleared the Man-track, scrabbled for a hold on the very tips of the branches of the tree opposite and hung there, repeating, "I beat the hound-dread, I beat the hound-dread, the hound-dread, hound-dread," and as her brain cleared and her breathing slowed, a new and beautiful figure formed in her mind – 100 – and she knew then that numbers went on for ever and ever!

Below her, bruised and bedraggled, Next-King Sallow crawled from the puddle in the Man-track into which he had fallen, and, shaking off the proffered paws of Woodlouze and Zpider, limped back to the east, coughing and spitting out the blood which bubbled up from his strained lungs and consigning all Westerners, and especially Marguerite, to the Sunless Pit.

Marguerite thanked the Sun for her escape but Oak and Old Burdock could not believe this would be the end of the affair.

The Bright One had recently taken to scratching numbers in the smooth bark of birch trees, 100, 101 . . . 123, 321 . . . finishing each session with her mark – X, until Burdock pointed out gently that as the trees grew the numbers would get bigger.

"Larger," Marguerite corrected her grandmother, equally gently, and tried to explain the difference when applied to numbers.

"Either way they disfigure the trees and that isn't done, my dear."

> *Squirrels protect trees.*
> *They have enough enemies,*
> *Treat them as our friends.*

So Marguerite went back to scratching in the sand on the beach, but if any piece of driftwood offered a clear surface it soon carried the marks of her claws and teeth. 123 X. 654 X. 666 X.

Chapter 21

A week had passed since the chase. The days were warmer, buds were breaking and leaves opening all over the island. Most of the western squirrels were out in the sunshine and many, led by Fern, were replacing the linings of their winter dreys or contemplating building lighter summer ones. There had been no word from the east, and none of the Royals, nor any of the zervantz, were coming to the teaching sessions any more.

A Council Meeting was held but there was little to discuss. There was an air of expectation, but none could think of any action that they could take to heal the breach between east and west. They would just have to wait and see what would happen. It was as if an invisible wall had been built from north to south across the middle of Ourland, the Royals and the zervantz rigidly confining themselves to the eastern end and leaving the exiles to their own devices in the west.

After the meeting, Marguerite was on the beach scratching figures in the sand, watched at a distance from downwind by Juniper. She moved to a clear patch, away from the scratch-marks she had just made, and found a most curious piece of driftwood washed up by the sea. It was almost the same size as herself and the sand-smoothed wood was twisted into a spiral where some creeper had once grown tightly around it. The creeper itself had been worn away by the action of the waves and the sand that had smoothed the wood. She bit the end to try and identify the wood. It looked to her like hazel and the taste should confirm this, but the expected nutty flavour had been leached out by the sea and replaced by salt. She spat out the bitter wood and rubbed her whiskers that were tingling in a strange way.

Digging into her memory Marguerite recalled the hazel sapling, strangled by a honeysuckle bine, that she had seen in the shaft of sunlight when she had been with Rowan at the Blue Pool so long, long ago. She looked across the water at the mainland and sniffed. Juniper moved a little closer.

Enough of this squimpish nostalgia, she thought and reached out to scratch a number on the smooth wood. As she touched the spiral, her whiskers tingled again as though the wood held some hidden power, and she pulled her paw away. The tingling stopped. She tried again, producing the same effect. Juniper crept a little closer, his nostrils twitching.

Marguerite reached out boldly, held the stem firmly with her left paw and cut 123456710 X deeply into the wood with her teeth, her whiskers buzzing wildly with excitement as she did so. Juniper hopped closer still.

There was still room for more figures on the smooth grey driftwood so Marguerite lightly scratched a 3 after the X.

She felt the surge of power that spiralled out of the end of the woodstock and twisted across the beach, bowling

Juniper over, before it dissipated above the sea, leaving him groaning and clutching at his face.

"Sun, my whiskers, Sun, my whiskers," he kept saying.

Marguerite ran to him and pulled his paws away. His whiskers were curled into spirals as tight as those on the twisted stick. She tried not to smile at his ludicrous appearance as she attempted, unsuccessfully, to comb them straight with her claws.

An hour later, at Juniper's insistence, Clover bit away each whisker, to stop the spinning feeling in his head.

Several more days passed with no word from the Easterners.

Juniper was recovering slowly as his whiskers started to regrow but he could not climb and was living in a ground-drey hidden in the bushes near the shore.

The Woodstock, left on the beach while Juniper was being attended to, had evidently floated away on the next tide. Marguerite searched for it each day, trying beach after beach all around the western end of Ourland.

"Why is it so important, my dear?" Old Burdock had asked.

"I don't know. I just know that I must find it. Will you help me?" They searched together in vain. Then, one evening, as the tide was going out, Marguerite, alone this time, was rummaging through the flotsam in a bay on the north-west corner of the island when, to her delight, she found the Woodstock again, lying half buried in the drying seaweed. She approached cautiously, reached out and touched it. Her whiskers tingled, and with mounting excitement, she again scratched a 3 after the 123456710 X.

The force spiralled out along the beach and she felt it fade away and die just beyond the water's edge. She tried a 6 and out over the sea in the line the force had taken, a group of seagulls rose in a twist from the water, calling angrily. A 1 produced no result at all, and the force produced by a 2 did not even reach the shoreline.

So intent was she with her experiments in the gathering dusk that she did not see the ancient, dingy-white squirrel hobbling towards her on the sand.

He called to her, "Yew, Yew."

She looked up in panic, pulled the Woodstock towards herself in a defensive gesture and scratched a 6 on the wood.

The surging, spiralling power caught the old squirrel and threw him on his back.

Marguerite ran from the beach as though all the foxes, dogs, martens and hawks in the world were after her.

In the calm of the morning she led others down to the shore, disturbing a pair of herring-gulls who had just pecked the pink eyes from The Nipper's body. No squirrel wanted to approach the corpse too closely, but despite their protests, Marguerite rolled the Woodstock to a place well above the tideline and then insisted that the body was decently buried under a tree, as was proper for any Sun-gone squirrel.

Chapter 22

Remembering the disparaging way in which King Willow had spoken of The Nipper, Burdock saw an opportunity to reinstate Marguerite in the King's favour and perhaps end the artificial partition of the island. She went off alone later that day to see him.

She was coolly received. Like herself, the King was ageing rapidly and Next-King Sallow was now always at his side. Both were seated high in the Royal Macrocarpa Tree, with its many great trunks, as she described what had happened at the North-West Bay.

The King listened with interest; he was really quite fond of this knowledgeable old Tagger as she called herself, and was about to say, "Fanzy The Nipper ztill being alive," when Next-King Sallow, his thin face cold with fury, said to Burdock, "Are yew telling uz that yewr granddaughter huz killed a Royal?"

"You could put it that way," she replied, "but . . ."

"No butz about it," said Next-King Sallow. "By yewr own admizzion her huz, and her muzt be tried for it." He turned to the King. "Tomorrow uz tryz her; uz – Zallow – will prozecute."

The King, with some reluctance, agreed, and said to Burdock, "Thiz iz the Law and at High Zun on the Morrow, Marguerite the Bright One muzt appear before the Royal Court. Her will be charged with 'Taking the Life of a Fellow Zquirrel, Knowing Him to be a Member of the Royal Family, the Punizhment for Which iz Tail-docking'."

Next-King Sallow slipped away through the branches, his skinny tail even higher than usual, knowing that once the Court had been declared it could not be cancelled.

A shocked Burdock tried to speak about it to the King. "But this is a nonsense," she started to say.

Embarrassed, the King cut her short. "Uz can't discuzz it with yew. That'z the Law," he said. "Yewr Marguerite muzd be here at High Zun. Her can have won other zquirrel with her, no more iz allowed."

Burdock was "dismizzed".

At the Westerners' Council Meeting she related what had happened.

"It's that Sun-damned squimp Sallow trying to get his own back," said Heather.

"That's obvious," replied Clover, "but what can we do about it?"

"Tell them to go to the Sunless Pit," said Tamarisk the Tactless, now a handsome yearling, though as quick with his tongue as ever.

"What are these trials like?" asked Larch the Curious. "I'd like to go to one."

"You can't," Burdock told him. "Only one other squirrel is allowed by their Law. We must decide who it is to be."

The choice came down to Oak, as Council Leader and Marguerite's father, or to Burdock as the Tagger, and because she had a greater knowledge of squirrel traditions than any of the others. Although, as she readily admitted, the Ourlanders' customs were different from those she knew so well.

Burdock skilfully guided the meeting to select her. She was thinking ahead.

At mid-morning on "the Morrow", Fern was trying to groom Marguerite's tail. "Appearances *are* important, my dear," she said as Marguerite pulled it away.

All the Westerners accompanied Marguerite and Old Burdock to the west–east boundary where Oak took Burdock to one side and pleaded with her. "Look after Marguerite, she means a lot to all of us."

"I know that," she told him. "I'll do all I can."

"Sun guide you both," they called after the Bright One and her grandmother as they watched them hop off down the Man-track to the trial. It seemed unfair to them that all the Easterners were allowed to attend, even the zervantz.

Clover slipped quietly away to look for a woundwort plant.

The Court was held in the upper branches of the Royal Tree. King Willow and Kingz-Mate Thizle each held a feather from one of the peacocks that strutted around the meadow behind the castle and Next-King Sallow held a white seagull quill which he waved in the air to emphasise any point he wanted to make. It all seemed somewhat bizarre to Burdock and Marguerite who were both used to more simple proceedings.

"Zilenze," said the King, waving his gaudy feather.

"It huz been reported to uz" – he glanced at Burdock, who shifted on the branch uncomfortably – "that yew, Marguerite, known as the Bright One, huz killed a Royal. Iz thiz true?" He pointed the feather at her.

"Yes, what happened was this – "

Next-King Sallow raised his quill to stop her.

"Yew admit killing Nipper the Royal?"

"Yes. But – "

"No butz! Yew are clearly guilty by yewr own admizzion. Yew knew it wuz wrong to kill a Royal?" He pointed the quill at her.

"It is wrong to kill any squirrel. What happened – " Marguerite started to reply, but Next-King Sallow cut her short with a wave of the quill.

"Thiz wuz not *any* zquirrel. Anzwer the queztion."

"What happened was this – "

She was cut short again. "Yew knew it wuz wrong to kill a Royal?"

Marguerite was getting angry. "Please. Will you listen to me? Please?" she shouted.

"Zllenze in the Court," ordered the King, waving his feather.

Burdock tried to intercede.

"Yew are only allowed here to zee, not to zay anything," Next-King Sallow told her and turned back to Marguerite.

"Do yew admit that yew killed Nipper the Royal and that yew knew it wuz wrong to kill a Royal?"

"Yes," she replied.

He spread his paws wide and said, "Yew have all heard her confezz," he said. "And by Ourland Law that iz the end

135

of it. A confezzion completez the trial. Uz demandz that the penalty iz paid. Tail-docking iz the decreed punizment." He turned to his father expectantly.

King Willow was looking out over the harbour, thinking, then, making up his mind said, "Killing any Royal iz a heinouz offenze and muzd be punizhed according to the Law. Tail-docking at dawn."

Burdock, who could not believe what she was hearing, leaned over to Marguerite and whispered, "When I say go, run. Hide by Pottery Point. There is no justice here." She turned to King Willow and eyed him coldly.

"What I have seen here today is a disgrace to Squirreldom. I demand the right to speak before any sentence is pronounced."

The King looked away towards the castle. "Yew are only here to zee. The Court iz over, zentenze huz been pronounzed. Tail-docking at dawn. However" – he paused and looked at Marguerite – "the prizoner iz allowed by our Law to make won ztatement, and won only." He signalled to her with the feather.

Marguerite looked at the distraught Burdock, drew herself up to her full height, raised her tail and spoke the Understanding Kernel.

If you could know all
Then you could understand all
Then you'd forgive all.

She looked expectantly at the King. He could not meet her eye and got up to leave with Kingz-Mate Thizle behind him, both awkwardly carrying their peacock feathers. As the other Royals and the zervantz lowered their tails in deference, Burdock leaned over to Marguerite and said, "Go. Go now!"

Somehow Old Burdock, despite her age, seemed to be everywhere and in every squirrel's way, jumping from one of the tree's many trunks to another and then another and back again. In the ensuing confusion Marguerite launched herself out of the Macrocarpa and into a chestnut tree. "One," she counted.

By the time pursuit had been organised she was six trees in front of the nearest chasers, the zervantz Woodlouze and Zpider, heading, as Burdock had suggested, for Pottery Point.

"7, 10, 11 . . . 65, 66, 67, 70 . . . " she counted as she jumped from tree to tree.

At the boundary she glanced back. She was still ahead of Woodlouze and Zpider by some 7 trees but, not far behind the two zervantz, she could hear the excited chatter of a mass of pursuing squirrels, with Next-King Sallow's high-pitched voice urging them on.

Then she heard Juniper's voice calling up from the ground below. "Go to the Woodstock Beach," he called. "I'll try and divert the others." He hid himself under a bush as Marguerite changed course. "532, 533, 534 . . ."

"Her'z heading for Pottery Point, her'z zinking fazt, uz'll catch her zoon," Juniper called up as the first two squirrels passed above him.

Woodlouze and Zpider ignored him, they had seen her alter course and ran on in hot pursuit.

Juniper was more successful with the mob. They heard the first lie he had ever told and headed south-west.

Marguerite was in fact "zinking fazt". Her energy, already drained by a sleepless night, the tension of her trial and the run through the trees in the heat of the day, was virtually exhausted.

"775, 776, 777." There was one more tree – and there was no number for it! She leapt for the tree, a pine, missed and fell to the beach. The Woodstock was somewhere ahead and she knew that she could get to it if she could only keep going through the sand, through the sand. She struggled on, "Through sand, through sand, throu'sand, th'ou'sand, thou'sand . . ."

Thousands of grains of sand scattered behind her as she made one last scrabbling attempt to stay ahead of the zervantz and reach the Woodstock.

Her sight was failing, her limbs were no longer obeying her brain and she knew then that she could not reach it before the zervantz caught up with her. But, as she lost consciousness, her last thought was that, if she had to lose her lovely tail, at least she had found the number which came after 777 – 1000. One thou'sand, one thousand, how beautiful it sounded.

She awoke to find Woodlouze and Zpider licking her face and paws and was surprised at their evident delight when she opened her eyes.

"Oh, ma'am, yew are awl right. Uz are zo pleazed," said Woodlouze.

"Yewr Juniper led the otherz away. Uz recognized hiz voize," added Zpider. "Yew're safe with uz for a bit."

Chapter 23

On a beach on the far side of Poole Harbour, the human holidaymakers were complaining about the heat. The scent of suntan lotion hung heavy in the sultry air. Instead of lying on their towels, people were holding them above their heads to act as sun-shelters. The temperature rose ever higher. Little whirlwinds raised spirals of dry sand which chased each other about the beach, stinging skin and eyes.

Some people were beginning to pack up and leave, although it was only mid-afternoon. Then, as though directed by some co-ordinating force, the little whirlwinds joined to make one big one which whooshed across the beach, filling the air with flying towels, sunhats and paper bags. A child's rubber dinghy was lifted high in the sky and dropped far out in the harbour to float away on the tide.

The holidaymakers, strangers until then, gathered in friendly groups to discuss the phenomenon and to sort their own belongings from the heaps scattered across the sand. Above the chatter a little boy's voice wailed, "Daddy, my boat's gone!"

When Juniper knew that the pursuing Easterners were at

Pottery Point, searching for Marguerite amongst the broken shards, he went as fast as he could with his half-grown whiskers, through the tangled rhododendron bushes, past the ruined Man-dreys of Maryland and on towards Woodstock Bay. He had to make sure that she had been able to use that weapon to deal with the two zervantz.

On the way he met Tamarisk.

"What's going on?" he asked.

As they ran together through the bushes, Juniper told Tamarisk of the trick he had played on the Easterners. Then, dropping down on to Woodstock Beach, they were very surprised to find Marguerite being cared for by the two zervantz who were tending her with every sign of affection.

They went across the sand to them, to ensure that she was safe.

We must get her off Ourland, Juniper was thinking, but it was Tamarisk who saw the red rubber dinghy drifting past. "Frizzle my whiskers," he said, "the Sun's-child is back."

Juniper looked up. "So it is," he said. Then, clutching at a leaf, "Maybe it's come to take Marguerite to safety."

"It's not coming in," said Tamarisk. "You're the Swimmer, you'll have to swim out and fetch it."

Juniper looked at the water, calm and blue under the bright Sun, took a deep breath, waded in and swam out strongly to the rubber boat. He gripped a rope that was hanging over the side with his teeth, and towed it ashore. Digging his claws into the sand, he tugged until one end of the boat was resting on the beach.

"Quick, get in," he told Marguerite, who had recovered

her composure. She started to climb the rope, then dropped back on to the sand.

"I'm taking the Woodstock," she said, "it's up there behind those stones." Together they rolled it down the beach and, by piling up other pieces of driftwood to make a ramp, they got it over the side and into the boat. Thinking that she might need it later, she asked them to throw the rest of the wood in after it.

Marguerite climbed the rope, followed by Woodlouze and Zpider.

"Uz can't ztay now," Woodlouze explained. "Next-King Zallow would have uz tailz. Or worze!" She shuddered.

Together Juniper and Tamarisk waded out, pushing the new Sun's-child into deeper water, then as a breeze caught it, Juniper climbed up the rope.

"Are you coming too?" Marguerite asked.

"Of course," Juniper answered.

"Help, help me, someone," called Tamarisk, and Juniper looked over the side to see him hanging on to the rope and being towed through the water as the new Sun's-child responded to the strengthening wind.

Together they hauled him aboard and he collapsed, spluttering, amongst the driftwood.

"It looks as if you're coming as well," said Marguerite.

"In for a hazelnut, in for a walnut. I've always wanted to go climbabout but there's nowhere new to go on that Sun-damned Ourland. So, what's to be seen?" He climbed up the pile of driftwood and peered towards the land. "Look at this," he called.

They were being blown along past Pottery Point. The

squirrels there had abandoned their search and were grouped on the beach, as Next-King Sallow, once again coughing up blood after the exertion of the chase, was giving orders for them to spread out through the trees and try to locate Marguerite by her scent-trail.

Tamarisk, balanced on the edge of the Sun's-child, thumbed his nose at the group, as he had once done at the Greys on the mud-flats, and called out across the water, "Who'z a zilly zquirrel, then?"

Next-King Sallow turned, saw the rubber boat carrying the fugitive Marguerite, that creep, Juniper, who always seemed to be wherever Marguerite was, another squirrel who was being openly insulting to his Royal Personage and, worst of all, two disloyal zervantz, all laughing at him.

He spluttered in fury, unable to find words. The sunlight was sparkling on the water, the reflections hurting his eyes. Uz'z not feeling well, he thought. The damned zun iz too hot. Uz *muzd* get into the zhade.

He started to move backwards, slipped on a shard covered in sea-slime, and fell, blood gushing scarlet from his mouth.

The fugitives were, by then, too far away to see this happen or to notice that no squirrel went forward to help the stricken Next-King; they just stood round in a circle and watched him die. When a bottle-blue fly, heavy with eggs, landed on the face of Never-to-be-King Sallow, and proceeded to lay the eggs in his mouth, no squirrel moved forward to flick it away.

They all looked at one another. *Someone* was going to have to tell the King.

Chapter 24

It was strange that no boats had come near the Sun's-child with the squirrels aboard. Each time a boat with its tall mast and bright sails had looked as though it *was* coming near, there had been a shift of the wind and it had turned about and sailed away again. The Sun's-child itself had been blown up and down the harbour but had never come near to land.

As the sun slipped below the western horizon, the wind fell away entirely and the light rubber dinghy bearing the five squirrels, the Woodstock and the pile of assorted driftwood was carried on the falling tide out towards the harbour entrance and the open sea. Brownsea Island had appeared to drift past them again in the near darkness, but they could see no sign of squirrel life on shore. Waves slapped against the boat's side as they were drawn along, the sounds magnified by the inflated rubber ring.

Then the Man-lights of the car ferry crossed in front of them, carrying the day's last load of vehicles and, feeling the lift and surge of the open sea, they were out into the swell of Poole Bay.

The squirrels did not sleep much that night. Marguerite

repeated an old Kernel to encourage them, suddenly feeling the weight of responsibility for others.

> *Have faith in the Sun*
> *His ways are mysterious.*
> *Faith can fell fir trees.*

Faith. Just have Faith. There was nothing else she could do. Just wait, watch and have Faith.

"Where are we?" Juniper asked, climbing up the driftwood to join Marguerite as the top rim of a huge red sun showed above the horizon. Around them gulls floated on the gently undulating sea, watching the dinghy with its unusual passengers.

"Sunknows," she replied. "Certainly not where I expected to be."

A light breeze ruffled her tail, held high so as not to convey her concern to the others below. She had been "sensing" the breeze to try and find which way it was blowing but it seemed to move about. Sometimes it came from the east, sometimes from the north and even on one occasion briefly from the south.

When the swell lifted them, land was visible far off to the west but hidden when they sank into the next trough, the movement leaving an uncomfortable feeling in Marguerite's stomach.

Woodlouze woke from a brief doze, nudged Zpider awake and apologised to Marguerite. "Uz be zorry, ma'am," she said, "uz haven't zeen to yewr breakfazt." Then, realising that there was no food on board, bowed her head in confusion. Zpider put his paw on Woodlouze's forearm.

Marguerite hopped down from the woodpile to where the two zervantz stood together.

"We have no food, but we are all well fed and can go for days without it if need be. We do in the winter, remember. And you mustn't call me ma'am. I am Marguerite. We are all friends here."

"Yez, ma'am," said Zpider and they all laughed.

"We must do something about *your* names too," she said, then added, "unless you like to be called Woodlouze and Zpider, that is."

"Zervantz iz alwayz called after creepy-crawliez," said Woodlouze.

"You aren't zervantz now, you are our friends and companions. Would you like new names?"

"Yez, pleaze, ma'am," they replied together.

"*Marguerite*," she corrected them. "Zpider, how would you like us to call you Spindle; that is a lovely tree to be named after. It has pink fruit and the leaves turn bright red in the autumn."

"Thank yew, ma'am, Marguerite ma'am, uz would like that. Zpindle, Zpindle, Zpindle," he said.

"And for you, Woodlouze, I would love to call you Wood Anemone. It is one of my favourite flowers; anemone means 'Flower of the Wind'."

'Oh ma'am, Marguerite uz meanz, that iz a nize name. Pleaze do alwayz call uz that," she said, her tail rising for the first time that she could remember.

After High Sun, Juniper, who was on watch on the driftwood pile, called down to Marguerite, "The land is getting closer!" and they all climbed up to see. To the west of them were white cliffs and they could see that some had been eroded by the sea to form high pillars of chalky rock.

By evening they were amongst these, being tossed about very uncomfortably by waves breaking around the bases of the rock columns. Above them cormorants and other seabirds were flying in to roost for the night.

"It's like being in a stone forest," said Tamarisk. "These are like great stone tree trunks."

"Hold on," shouted Juniper, when an especially large wave nearly tipped them over as it smashed against the foot of one of the pillars and, turning over backwards, soaked the squirrels with spray. He eyed the sharp-pointed barnacles under the seaweed apprehensively, knowing how easy it was to pierce a Sun's-child's skin. If that happened it would be the end of them all.

"Trust in the Sun. Trust in the Sun," Marguerite kept telling the frightened squirrels in her care, but as the sun itself disappeared behind the cliffs, and the frail craft was tossed about in the surges, even she was losing a little of her faith. "Trust in the Sun. Faith can fell fir trees," she told herself, wishing that she was in a snug drey high in a fir tree right now. Calling to Tamarisk to take over the watch, she dropped down to comfort Wood Anemone and Spindle below. Juniper, with his short whiskers, was having a bad time balancing and was feeling very sick.

Marguerite was with the ex-zervantz, whispering, "Trust in the Sun," to each squirrel, when she became aware of something quite outside her experience.

Her ears heard whistles, grunts and clicks coming through the water which reverberated in the hollow air-filled rubber tube of the Sun's-child, but her mind heard something quite different. Two voices, one clearly male and the other female, were debating an issue in voices as soft and as sweet as breezes in high pines.

"I think we will have to modify that ancient Great Explosion theory. Since the South Atlantic Right whales found those strange holes in the atmospheric ozone it is much easier for them to pick up the signals placing the Black Holes. Thinking about the Universal Origins, now I believe that matter has *always* existed. It's more logical for the Universe to be expanding and then contracting in waves over enormous periods of time; from a Great Explosion and an outward wave, then a slowing-down of expansion, then an ever-increasing contraction, then another Great Explosion and off we go again. I never could accept that everything suddenly came into existence in one flip.

"That would make us now, as a mere planet in this Universe, be swimming outwards on a wave from the centre . . ."

The voice stopped. Then –

"Malin, some mammal is praying, we must help."

"You're right, Lundy. Near Finfast Point amongst the rock pillars. Mammals – I sense them to be squirrels, like the ones we saw down the coast – in danger. Turn and follow!"

A minute later, with the clicking and grunting now audible to all the squirrels, the heads of two dolphins broke the surface, one on either side of the Sun's-child.

Marguerite and Juniper had joined Tamarisk on the woodpile and looked with amazement at the strange creatures in the water.

In her mind Marguerite heard one dolphin say to the other, "Underneath and nose away."

An air of great peace and protection came over them. The dolphins' blowholes closed, their black polished heads slid below the surface, and the Sun's-child moved effortlessly away from the rocks and into the safety of the open Sea.

The heads popped up again. "Where are you going?" the soughing sound in her head asked, more or less in time with the movement of Malin's mouth.

Anywhere safer than this, Marguerite thought, but before she could speak the words, the dolphins seemed to understand.

"We know a place where other squirrels live. By the Sea. Would you like to go there?" a voice in her head asked.

"What colour are they?" Marguerite did not have to speak.

"An animal's colour means nothing to us, but their shape and size is the same as yours."

"Are their ears round or pointed?"

"The same as yours."

"Then we would like to go to them."

Marguerite realised that she had not opened her mouth and the other squirrels were looking at her with puzzled expressions on their faces.

The dolphins slid down and under the Sun's-child and propelled it gently southwards, taking it in turns to rise for air, all the time soundlessly conversing with Marguerite.

"We can't take you all the way, but we can put you into currents that will. We will put you at the end of the

148

Current ⋈ 3* and that will take you to 3 ⋈ 3 then 3 ⋈ 33. Current ⋈ 4 will take you ashore."

The dolphins read Marguerite's incomprehension. "Don't worry, trust in your Sun. You will be safe."

"How can you be sure?"

"Some of us have learned to 'Look Forward', but we don't often do that, it makes us sad. We learn to 'Look Backwards' even before we are born. We know the history of our race, back as far as when we lived on the land as you do still. Then we learn to 'Look Round' and find out all we can about Now and Here. Malin and I are studying 'Look Out' – searching way, way beyond this our planet 'Water'. It is most interesting but can be brain-exhausting. We are on our way to meet others near the Goodwin Sands to share our ideas. We often school there together."

"Can you count numbers?" Marguerite asked.

There was a pause. Then, "Count yours to us."

Marguerite started, "1, 2, 3, 4, 5, 6, 7, 10, 11 . . . "

"Ahhhh, yes, Base Eight, humans use Base Ten now. When we first taught the Phoenicians they used Base ⋈ like us. That would be 60 in human numbers and" – there was a momentary pause – "74 in yours."

"Do *you* teach humans?"

"We used to, when they would listen. We had high hopes for them. They still use our ⋈ for counting their time and 6 ⋈ for dividing up circles, but they have probably forgotten where they learned it. With ten digits on their hands, Base Ten is easier for most of them."

"Don't they listen now?"

* ⋈ is pronounced Zix-T

"Sadly no, they have been conceit-deaf for more than ⚲ of our generations."

The soughing in Marguerite's head died away, and the Sun's-child slowed to a stop. The dolphins' heads appeared above the water.

"We have brought you to Current ⚲ 3. You will be with the others of your kind by dawn on the day following tomorrow. We must leave you now. Dolphins must always be on time!

> *Punctuality*
> *Is vital. Other's time wasted,*
> *Is stolen by you*
> *And can never be returned.*
> *Lost minutes sink for ever.*

"Farewell, our friends, we are glad we heard your prayer."

They dived, then leapt together in a glorious arc through the air and swam off up-channel in the gathering darkness, followed by the unspoken but received thanks of Marguerite.

After the dolphins had gone, she felt unutterably lonely despite the presence of the other squirrels, who seemed not to have understood any of the conversation. She tried to explain to them what the dolphins had told her.

Chapter 25

The circle of silent zervantz surrounding the body of Sallow widened to allow Next-King Poplar through. He ordered them to carry the fly-blown corpse of his brother back to the Royal Macrocarpa Tree, following the cortège himself at a distance.

Poplar, attending the Court at High Sun, had listened to the proceedings with dismay. Everything that he had heard and seen had been contrary to what he had been taught by Old Burdock during the previous year, when he had studied Squirrel Lore and Traditions with the incomers.

> Squirrels have the right
> To explain their own actions,
> Fully – in silence.

Marguerite had not been allowed to do this. It was plainly unjust. Then there was:

> Punishment through pain
> Degrades the one who gives – more
> Than the receiver.

His brother had been spared this degradation, thank the Sun. Now it was going to be up to him to tell the King – and the Kingz-Mate.

These low-tailed zervantz were having the distasteful job of carrying his brother's body the full length of Ourland because he, another squirrel like them, had ordered them to do so.

Each squirrel is Free
To choose its own root through Life –
Guided by Kernels.

Sallow's corpse was laid at the foot of the Royal Tree and Next-King Poplar climbed up to tell his father of the circumstances of his brother's death, as told to him by the zervantz who had been present.

The King was silent for a while. He looked tired and old, all his pride and arrogance gone. He stared at his youngest son, sitting, head bowed and tail low, on the branch before him. For the first time in his life, he saw that Poplar was a fitter and better squirrel than Sallow had ever been.

He looked out over the sea, then, appearing to have come to some great decision, called for his and the Kingz-Mate's peacock feathers to be brought to them, together with one more. He stood to his full height, a Royal and dominating figure again, held his tail high and announced, "Uz *lazt* Decree iz thiz – uz giv'z up uz Kingz-zhip irrevocably and pazz thiz Name, the Dutiez and the Privilegez on to uz zun, King Poplar the Zixth. Long live King Poplar."

He bit through his peacock feather and let the pieces fall

through the branches to the ground far below, then looked expectantly at the Kingz-Mate, who, with just a hint of reluctance, did the same with hers, watching the blue and green feather, gleaming bright in the evening sun, drift away on a light breeze.

The Ex-King lowered his tail, handed the new feather to King Poplar the Zixth and turned to leave. His head was aching and he wanted to lie down, away from the excited chatter that had followed his announcement.

"Wait," commanded the new King. "Uz *firzt* Decree iz thiz. All zervantz are free," and, before any squirrel could realise the significance of this, he declared, "And uz zecond, and *lazt* Decree iz to abolizh for ever in Ourland the pozition and rank of King." He bit through his feather and let the pieces drop.

"In future uz am to be known az Poplar; not King Poplar, not even Ex-King Poplar, juzt Poplar."

In the chill of the following morning, Juzt Poplar crossed the west—east boundary, abolishing it with a flick of his tail to the cheers of a gaggle of adoring ex-zervantz who were busy trying to keep their tails in unaccustomed upright positions.

Behind them came Ex-King Willow playing hide and seek in the bushes with the dreylings of the ex-zervantz, and a slightly huffy Ex-Kingz-Mate.

"Uz haven't enjoyed uzzelf zo much for yearz," he told her.

Oak, Burdock and the rest of the exiles were in the trees above Woodstock Bay, looking out over the harbour.

Tansy had seen the Sun's-child leaving on the tide, and they were hoping it would return, unaware of what had taken place at Pottery Point, or later at the Royal Tree. They were now huddled together awaiting events when they heard the joyous group approaching.

"Will *you* be our Leader?" Juzt Poplar called up to Oak.

"That depends," Oak replied cautiously, and came down the trunk to learn from Poplar of the unexpected and dramatic events that had occurred at the eastern end of the island.

Old Burdock went across and brushed whiskers with Ex-King Willow and Ex-Kingz-Mate Thizle.

"Long live a united Ourland!" she said, and each squirrel repeated the words.

Chapter 26

Marguerite suggested to the squirrels below that they come up and lick some of the condensed dew from the Sun's-child's skin before the sun rose and dried it up. The sky was clear and it was going to be another hot day with no more water for them until nightfall.

Just before dawn a sleek warship had passed at a distance, leaving her wondering what the straight horizontal branches were that she could see silhouetted against the sky. She marvelled too at seeing some of *her* numbers painted hugely on its side: F126. The F puzzled her, but the numbers were hers.

The rubber dinghy was too small to show on the ship's radar but the pinging of its Asdic transmissions, as it sensed for hidden submarines, was picked up by the squirrels' sensitive whiskers, the pulses amplified by the inflated ring of the Sun's-child.

If it is trying to talk to us, thought Marguerite, I understood the dolphins better. Perhaps it's a special language these great ships use to each other when they are offering help.

*

Throughout the long day, the land to the north slipped past as they were carried along on the sea's currents. Now and then the flow would appear to stop and the Sun's-child would circle aimlessly for a few minutes, then they would be caught by another current and drawn off in a slightly different direction, sometimes close to the cliffs, sometimes well out to sea, but always westwards.

Another night crept up on them from the east and the squirrels settled down to try and sleep. The Sun had dried up the sea-water that had splashed into the Sun's-child before the dolphins came, so they were dry and more comfortable now, although very hungry. All of them, including Juniper, had adjusted to the rising and falling motion of the sea.

During the night a wind from the south-west started to blow, gently at first, then growing in strength until, by midnight, it was driving them rapidly towards the shore. A fitful moon came out from behind the clouds and showed Marguerite the dangers that lay ahead. On Ourland she had often heard waves rushing at the shore and watched them curling over in a mass of white froth and bubbles. She knew that this was happening now, somewhere in front of them, and as the sounds were getting louder, she also knew that soon they would be in the breakers. "Trust in the Sun."

She turned to warn the others and found herself saying in a strong, confident voice:

> *Be ready to swim*
> *Keep together. Fear nothing.*
> *We will all be saved.*

Juniper added, "Trust in the Sun," as a giant wave lifted the Sun's-child, tipped it over in the surf and tumbled the squirrels into the cold water. Tamarisk, Spindle and Wood Anemone scrabbled and clutched at pieces of the driftwood thrown into the sea with them, while Marguerite swam directly to the shore.

Juniper, struck on the head by the Woodstock as the craft overturned, sank, and then, when he had struggled to the surface, found that he was trapped under the upturned Sun's-child, paddling round and round with no way of escape. In the blackness he felt the floating spiral of wood and grabbed at it in panic, his paws scratching and clawing at the smooth surface. He never knew which of Marguerite's numbers he unwittingly drew in the confusing darkness, but a powerful burst of energy shot out of the Woodstock, ripping the skin of the Sun's-child apart with an explosion that was heard by the other squirrels, now huddled together on the wet shingle further along the beach.

Coughing and spitting salt water, he climbed through the hole in the wet rubber and, as the current drew the remains of the dinghy along the shore, he swam through the breakers to the land, guided by the weak moonlight.

Chapter 27

Juniper was lying exhausted amongst the seaweed on the high-tide mark. Near him were the remains of the Sun's-child and at his side was the sodden Woodstock. A red squirrel with only a stump of a tail was shaking his shoulder. "Wake up, my friend, wake up," he was saying.

He rolled over in the soft light of the early dawn. A herring-gull was calling from a rock and the sound of the breakers was faint in his ears. He could just make out a sucking sound as the waves of the ebbing tide drew the shingle back after the rush up the beach.

Juniper coughed, tasting the salt in the fur around his mouth.

"Where are the others?" he asked.

"Don't worry, they are all safe, further along," the stump-tailed one said. "That bossy female sent me to find you."

Juniper smiled to himself, then looked ruefully at the remains of the Sun's-child. The stranger was nosing at the Woodstock. "Don't touch that!" Juniper called to him.

"Poisonous?" asked the stump-tailed one.

"No. I'll explain later," he said. "Could you take me to Marguerite, please?"

"I think we've met before," Juniper said, as he limped stiffly along the beach. "Didn't you come through our Guardianship with a group of refugees last summer? One of us, Clover the Carer, bit off your broken tail for you."

"Where was that?" asked Stump-Tail. "My memory of that terrible journey is all mixed up in my mind. We came through many Guardianships to end up here."

"Mine was Humanside, at the Blue Pool."

"Not that beautiful place with water the colour of a summer sky? Your Council Leader asked us to stay but we came on. I remember it now. How is Clover? I didn't see her with the others."

They joined Marguerite, Tamarisk and the ex-zervantz, who were sitting grooming themselves in the sunshine and talking to the refugees. They had washed away the salt and drunk deeply from a stream which ran down the valley before disappearing under the shingle at the top of the beach. Now their fur was nearly dry.

Marguerite hopped over to Juniper and brushed whiskers with him. "Are you all right?" she asked.

Juniper looked around guiltily, lowered his voice and said, "I killed the Sun's-child."

"You'd better tell me about it." Marguerite led him away to the stream and, as he washed and drank, she listened as he told her what he could remember of the incident in the surf.

"I heard the noise as I came ashore. I wondered what it was, there was no thunder in the sky. That was the Sun's-child dying?"

"Yes," said Juniper. "It was an accident. I touched the Woodstock by mistake in the darkness. I would have drowned if I had stayed under there much longer."

> *You are forgiven*
> *The Sun's-child died to save you*
> *Your life is needed.*

Marguerite looked around, as if to see who was speaking, then apologised to Juniper. "Sometimes it is as if someone else is speaking through my mouth."

Juniper looked at the bright-eyed squirrel with awe.

Stump-Tail and his party were exchanging stories of hazardous journeys with Marguerite and her companions.

Marguerite had counted the refugees. There was one lot of eight and four more – 14.

"What are your plans now?" Stump-Tail's life-mate, Dandelion, asked.

"We'll rest for a while with you if we may, and work out what to do next. We didn't *plan* this journey."

> *To make the Sun laugh*
> *You tell it, in detail, your*
> *Plans for your Future.*

They all smiled at this Kernel. Then she told the incredulous refugees of all that had happened on Ourland, culminating in their departure from there, and their arrival here, at what they learned was called Worbarrow Bay.

In turn, they heard of the adventures of the refugees when they had followed the Leylines to the coast.

"We must get the Woodstock," said Tamarisk after they had finished, and he started off along the beach.

"Wait," called Juniper after him, "I'll do that."

A crestfallen Tamarisk came back to the group and Juniper went to fetch their weapon, circling around the skin of the Sun's-child cautiously before returning, dragging the Woodstock in his teeth and keeping his paws well clear of the twisted section with the incomprehensible "numbers".

"Where are your dreys?" Marguerite asked Dandelion.

"We don't have any," she replied. "When we got here, at first we thought we were safe and built homes in the trees up the valley where the empty Man-dreys are. Then the Greys came and we were forced to leave."

"What are these empty Man-dreys?" asked Juniper.

"Where humans used to live, but they are like our old dreys now, falling to pieces."

"Perhaps other fierce humans came and drove out the humans who lived there," said Juniper.

"I don't think humans are like that," said Marguerite, remembering the Red-Haired Girl, the Human Who Picked Things Up and the Visitors at the Blue Pool. "I'm *sure* that it couldn't have been that."

"Where *do* you live, then?" asked Tamarisk.

"Up there," said Stump-Tail, waving his paw at the towering grass-covered mound of Worbarrow Tout which projected into the sea, surrounded by water on three sides. "In old rabbit holes," he added, his tail stump dropping in shame.

"Rabbit holes?" said Tamarisk, tactless as ever. "*Rabbit holes?*"

"Up there and on the beach are the only places where the Greys never come, so that's why we live *there*. We scavenge along the beach. You can get quite fond of seafood," said Stump-Tail. "Can't you, Dandelion-Mate?"

"I do still crave a pine kernel," she said. "You didn't bring any with you, I suppose?"

"Sorry," said Juniper. "Never a one."

"When you've eaten, would you like to join us in our holes?" asked Stump-Tail, remembering the rules of hospitality.

All passing strangers
Must be accommodated
At whatever cost.

"It is a long time since I heard that one," replied Marguerite, thinking of Marble's first visit. "Yes. We would be honoured, but please, we are old friends, not strangers," and she stepped forward and to their amazement brushed whiskers Ourland style with all the refugees. "Let's find food together."

As each of them moved away to forage on the beach, with Marguerite guiding them away from the remains of the Sun's-child, a pretty female squirrel approached her shyly. "I don't suppose you will remember me. My name is Meadowsweet. Where is your brother, Rowan the Bold? He's not with you?"

Marguerite turned her head away, then turned back and faced Meadowsweet. "It's rather a sad story," she said. "Can I tell you later?"

Chapter 28

A few days of recuperation followed, Marguerite and her party living amicably with Stump-Tail and the other coast-dwelling squirrels, but longing to get their claws into some tree-bark again. They felt safe enough living in the rabbit holes on Worbarrow Tout and all enjoyed the views over the sea, and of the white cliffs behind them, when on fine days they lay on rock-ledges in the sunshine, glad to be out of the dim burrow-light.

According to the coast-dwellers, humans only came there on two days each week and then they mostly stayed on the beach, very few climbing the steep path to the top of the Tout. The humans were easy for the squirrels to avoid, but it was not a life that any of them could see as a permanent arrangement. Squirrels *need* trees.

Marguerite sat in the sunshine thinking. Stump-Tail was obviously the Senior Squirrel, yet he was not now taking the lead in organising and guiding the group, and the lack of leadership was showing in many little ways – minor quarrels, a feeling of lassitude, morbid nostalgia and most of all a feeling that each day was somehow wasted. Yet he had brought his party safely to this place over the last year, so he must have the right qualities. Perhaps, through having no tail, he felt inhibited or insecure when it came to relationships with her party?

Then there was her own position to consider. Increasingly she wanted to spend time thinking; there was so much in the world that she did not understand and the day-to-day planning disrupted her contemplation. She would love to be a Tagger, she thought.

A good Leader needed a thinker behind him, one who had experienced real difficulties and had overcome them, someone who was respected as a "doer", as well as a "thinker", someone whose recommended tags would be recognised by all as fair and true, be they good or bad.

Was *she* up to this role? She was young for a Tagger and had not even mated yet. But then she seemed to command respect even from much older squirrels. The decision would not be hers anyway; all appointments had to be agreed by the group as a whole. But some squirrel would have to initiate the proceedings. *That* would have to be arranged.

Accordingly she suggested to Stump-Tail that they all get together that evening in Council to discuss plans for the future. He readily agreed and, as the day started to cool, the entire party gathered and sat in the sunshine amongst the sea-pinks and tufts of coarse grass on the top of the Tout, a pleasant sea breeze ruffling their fur and tails.

Marguerite waited for Stump-Tail to commence but he appeared reluctant to make the first move and looked towards her expectantly.

She glanced round, drew a deep breath and said, "*We* have called this meeting to draw up some plans for the future:

Squirrels without aims
Drift through life, vulnerable
To each passing whim.

"And for a group of squirrels to have no aims leaves us exposed to many kinds of danger. I would like to suggest that we choose who is to be our Leader and confirm *him* in that position, then discuss and select a Tagger from amongst ourselves. After that we can decide what our group aims should be. I propose that our friend without a tail be Leader of us all."

Marguerite turned and apologised for not having remembered his *real* name. Since they had been there he had always been called Stump-Tail.

"It's Alder," he told her. "Alder – with the stump-tail."

She recognised that he had said that to cover her embarrassment. It confirmed her belief that he had the sensitivity to be a good Leader, if only he also had the confidence.

"I propose our friend Alder Stump-Tail to be our Leader," Marguerite said again.

There was general agreement, shown by head-noddings and tail-twitchings from the squirrels.

Alder looked pleased, and, unable to give the tail-flick which says "I am willing to accept", bowed his head in an unmistakable gesture of acceptance.

Marguerite waited for Alder to propose a Tagger. In the silence that followed she realised that none of the coast-dwellers had tags; perhaps they had never had tags, and Taggers, at Wolvesbarrow. She glanced appealingly at Juniper the Swimmer.

165

Juniper drew himself up. "Not only does a group need a wise and steadfast Leader, it also needs a wise and thoughtful Tagger to advise the Leader, teach the dreylings and act as the conscience of the group by allocating tags to each, fairly and fearlessly. *We* have amongst us one such squirrel. I propose Marguerite the Bright One as our Tagger." He flicked his tail, and the others all followed.

Dandelion said, "We didn't have Taggers at our old home. We used to have a wise one whom we called the Bard, who acted as adviser to the Leader; but he was killed by a Grey just before we left and we haven't appointed another, what with one thing and another. I know that we'd all be happy to have Marguerite the Bright One as Bard and Tagger."

Marguerite raised her tail with the exact amount of speed and angle which indicated "I accept, with modesty, and thank you all for the trust you have put in me." There was no need to say it in words.

What she did say was, "Squirrels without tags are not complete squirrels. They have nothing to live up to, or master, and others do not know what to expect of them. If I may use our Leader, Alder, as an example?" She looked at him and he nodded. "While we call him Stump-Tail that will seem to be the most important thing about him and *he* will always be aware of it. Yet he led an entire party safely through many hazardous adventures to reach here. With the power you have given me I award him the tag Who Led His Party to Safety and we will call him simply Alder the Leader. Now it is up to him to take command and guide us wisely. I know that he will have the support of us all."

As she said this, Alder appeared to grow two inches in

height, and his lack of a tail faded into insignificance. He stepped forward, brushed whiskers with Marguerite the Tagger in the way she had taught him, and then confidently took over the meeting.

"Right," he said, "let's discuss what we should be doing, as self-respecting squirrels . . ." and the group, now united, discussed the options open to them.

It was agreed that they could not stay on the Tout. Spring was turning to summer, the flower heads on many of the tufts of sea-pinks were already brown and crisp. Speckled young gulls had left their cliff-face nests and were raucously demanding food from their parents as they sat on the rocks, beaks open to the sky. Yet no squirrel had felt the mating urge and this was a sure Sun-sign that things were not right for them there.

Inland were Greys who had forced them down from the abandoned Man-drey area to this treeless mound of Worbarrow Tout, where they had survived on seafood and by living in rabbit holes. If they were to hold their tails high again they must live, as squirrels, in trees. But where?

As far as they knew, the whole inland area was held by the Greys, and Ourland was a long way off and too dangerous for Marguerite and her party to return to, even if they could.

"We must remember that we have the Woodstock," she told them, "so the Greys won't have it all their own way. If we learn to use that effectively we could win back and hold an area for ourselves. With the Sun's help," she added.

"It would be a dangerous venture, we could all be killed," said Alder.

"That's true," said Marguerite, "and no squirrel should

be forced to join such an expedition, but to stay here means a degraded life with no future generations to follow."

Into her mind came a Sun-inspired picture of a lake of blue water sparkling in the bright morning light and she could smell the scent of warm pine bark and resin.

"Let's go and win back the Blue Pool," she said.

Chapter 29

The group, now working happily together, were resting on the top of Flowers Barrow, exhausted from the climb up the cliff-face.

Juniper had practised long and hard with the Woodstock, learning the numbers that had to be written after Marguerite's X to produce waves of different power and intensity. The beach below was littered with splintered pieces of wood that he had used as targets and the thistles on the bank behind were now trying to grow straight again. Having witnessed what it could do, all the other squirrels were now more confident of the success of their venture.

They had probed a little way inland along the stream from which they normally drank, and the only sign of Greys was a decomposing body in the stream itself. They each drank their fill, upstream from the body, watching, listening and scenting for the enemy, and then retreated up on to the Tout again. They would leave at first light and climb the Great Cliff to get to open ground where there would be less chance of meeting Greys. From the top, Dandelion, who was known to be the best at reading the Leylines, would guide them to the Blue Pool.

There had been almost a party atmosphere, a hint of squirrelation, as they had set off at daybreak along the beach to the undercliff, the older ones taking it in turns to drag the Woodstock. But, not being used to moving with a load, they had underestimated the time needed and it was High Sun before they were over the banks of fallen chalk and at the foot of the near-vertical cliff-face ready for the climb.

Juniper and Tamarisk had reconnoitred the face the previous evening, deciding that if they could find a path up, it would be safer than using the Man-track that led up from the valley to the Barrow of the Flowers, close to the edge of the cliff. A Grey attack there, with the cliff behind them and no known retreat route, would not be easy to hold off.

Juniper told Tamarisk:

> *In a strange country,*
> *Be careful. Time spent looking*
> *Is seldom wasted.*

"Not *exactly* appropriate for us now, but the message is right. That is one of the Kernels the Tagger teaches before you go on climbabout."

"This is much more exciting than climbabout," Tamarisk said to him as they had searched for a path to take them to the top.

The route they had found zigzagged up the face perilously, in places so narrow that the Woodstock had had to be dragged end-first with a danger that it might roll over the edge if they let go of it for a moment. Teeth and claws were aching from holding and pulling.

Squirrels ordinarily have no fear of heights up to that of the tallest tree, and they have sharp claws to grip fibrous bark, but climbing a cliff of crumbly white chalk while dragging the Woodstock was an altogether different experience.

They all found the great height brought on dizziness, and Marguerite advised them to keep their eyes on the path and not to look down. The sun, bright on the white chalk when they started their climb, obligingly hid behind a veil of thin cloud so they no longer had to half close their eyes, but seabirds, wheeling in to inspect the strange procession climbing up *their* cliff, screeched at them and sometimes nearly brushed the squirrels off the narrow pathway with their wing tips.

Where the ledge widened slightly near the top, they paused for breath. Marguerite ignored her own advice and peered over the edge to where the sea lay wrinkled far beneath them, patterned by darker stripes where currents ran. Her head swam and she felt dizzy. "Don't look down," she reminded herself. "Trust in the Sun."

Juniper was some way behind, helping Meadowsweet to pass a narrow place that sloped dangerously and where there were loose particles of chalk on the path.

"Can we rest here?" she pleaded when they came to a wider place.

Juniper stopped. The others were ahead but were still in sight, so would not be worrying about them. He was glad of the break too.

Meadowsweet looked at the older squirrel and said, "Would you tell me about Rowan the Bold leading the dreadful Greys away, and saving you all?"

Juniper smiled to himself. He had overheard Meadowsweet ask each of his party to tell her the same story whenever she could get one apart from the others. Having lost his own life-mate to the Greys he understood her feelings.

"Rowan the Bold was a hero," he told her. "There we were, up this fir tree which leant out over a clay-pan with 'lots' of Greys all around us on the ground. There was *no* way we could have escaped. Old Burdock, our Tagger, was exhausted, the rest of us were frightened, we had youngsters with us and no squirrel knew what to do. Then your Rowan crept craftily down the trunk so they could not see where he had come from, and shouted insults at the Greys.

"The whole horde of them ran off after him over the Great Heath, and he must have led them right into a fire, for they never came back. So we escaped and got away to Ourland.

"It was the bravest thing I have ever seen. I would have been proud to have had him for *my* son."

Meadowsweet looked proud herself, her bushy tail rising.

"Do you have any sons?" she asked Juniper.

"No," he replied, "my Bluebell and I were not Sun-blessed that way." He looked out over the sea to where the Isle of Portland lay low in the haze on the far horizon. "It's time we caught up with the others."

"What do you call this place?" Marguerite asked Alder.

They were enjoying the cool evening breeze which was blowing over the grass-covered hilltop.

"This is the Barrow of the Flowers," he replied.

"I can see the flowers," Marguerite said, looking around at the early harebells and the stemless thistles. "What's a barrow?"

"It's a place where the Ley forces start," replied Alder.

Marguerite looked puzzled. "Tell me more about these Ley forces."

"Don't you know about Leylines?" he asked. "How do you find your way about the country?"

"Until last year we had always lived at the Blue Pool and didn't need to. Will you tell me about them?"

"Not all squirrels can read the lines. I can, just, but Dandelion is very good at it. She grew up near the Barrow of the Wolves way up north of here in a big pine forest. There aren't any wolves there now but the name lingers on. I think that if you grow up near a barrow then you become extra sensitive. See if *you* can feel anything here."

He turned his head slowly. "There's a line," he said, "and there's another. There's the one we came in on last year." He pointed to the north. "There are a couple of others further round. Here's a very strong line. Try this one."

Marguerite sat up and turned in the direction indicated. She could see nothing nor sense anything unusual. The others of her party tried sensing in turn. Spindle, normally rather taciturn, called out excitedly, "Uz can feel it, uz can feel it. Uz whizkerz iz telling uz the line."

"How does it feel?" asked Juniper.

"Uz can't really dezcribe it, uz juzt knowz it'z there. And there, and there'z won there." He pointed to the north and then to the north-west.

Juniper tried, but with his whiskers still not fully regrown, he couldn't sense anything. Where he sat was a cigarette-end thrown down by a human earlier that day. The acrid scent was filling his nostrils, reminding him of the times when he and Bluebell had scavenged under the tables at the Eating Man-Drey. He hopped away and looked out over the vastness of the sea. "Bluebell," he sighed, "where are you now?"

Grasshoppers chirruped in the evening sunshine.

"Which way is it to the Blue Pool?" Marguerite asked Dandelion.

"Well, if you were to retrace the Leylines we took, you would go north to the Barrow of the Ferns, then turn away a bit to the Water Barrow, then north-east across a big heath to the Drinking Barrow and up to the barrow where we met the Three Lords."

"Who in the Sunless Pit are the Three Lords?" asked Tamarisk.

"We got to this particular barrow and I could feel a very strong force from the east, strong enough for several barrows together," said Dandelion. "We were going to go that way when three Greys appeared. They stopped us and wouldn't let us pass. The chief one called himself Lord Obsidian and the others were Lord Malachite and Lord Silicon. They said they were going to kill us but we pleaded with them and in the end they agreed to spare us if we turned south-west and didn't stop until we reached the sea. Mind you, we didn't really know what the sea was then. We do now, though!"

"Which way is it from the Three Lords Barrow to the Blue Pool?" asked Marguerite, her mind focused on their mission.

"South-east to the Icen Barrow, then pick up the force towards the mound where 'lots' of humans live. The one with the broken Man-drey on. That line passes right across your pool."

"We leave in the morning," Alder announced firmly. "We'll find shelter in a rabbit hole for tonight."

Chapter 30

When they were all huddled together cosily in the abandoned rabbit warren near the top of the Barrow of the Flowers, Marguerite asked Dandelion to tell them more about the Leylines. Dandelion knew lots of old legends and stories going back as far as the time of Acorn, the first squirrel, and loved to tell them to anyone ready and willing to listen. She only needed the slightest encouragement to launch into a story.

"And thereby hangs a tale," she would say. "Once upon a time . . ."

As the other squirrels jostled for position around Dandelion, Marguerite smiled as she recalled overhearing that "squamp" Tamarisk entertaining a group of yearlings one afternoon a week ago on the Tout below.

"Once upon a branch," he had started, mimicking Dandelion's Wolvesbarrow accent perfectly, "sat Acorn, the first squirrel in the world, holding a Council Meeting, all by himself, when he broke the first wind in the world. He looked round to see where it had come from. 'And thereby hangs a tail,' he said to himself."

There had been a snigger from his audience.

Marguerite had called to him quietly, but loud enough for the other yearlings to hear, "Tamarisk, when you grow out of being the Tactless I hope that I don't have to tag you the Rude Mimic."

There had been silence from the other side of the rock.

Now, with the whole group listening, Dandelion was in full voice.

"I think that the Leylines must always have been there, but my grandfather told me that *he* had been told that it was the humans who made them work many, many generations ago. They built the barrows on top of the hills and then smaller ones along the lines that appeared. Sometimes they made cones of soil which have since been flattened by the weather into low mounds; often they stood great stones up on end, sometimes they planted beautiful groups of pine trees on hilltops, but always on the Ley-force lines which are absolutely straight."

"Always?" asked Marguerite, fascinated by a subject so new to her.

"Always, absolutely," replied Dandelion. "Then, to move about the country through the trees, they followed the Leylines from marker to marker. In those days, my grandfather said, the whole country was covered in trees. A squirrel could go from the sea to the sea and never touch ground!"

"Do humans use them now?' Marguerite asked.

"I don't think so, they seem always to follow paths if they're walking, or roadways when they go about in groups in those smelly things. I think they've forgotten Leylines. I don't believe they even use them for sending messages now."

"Messages?" Marguerite's ears pricked up.

"That's another thing my grandfather told me. He was a wonderful old squirrel, what he didn't know wasn't worth knowing. I learned so much from him."

"Tell us about the messages," Marguerite said eagerly.

"When humans wanted other people to know something and did not want to walk there and tell them, they would go up to a high barrow and make special thoughts, facing along the Leyline the way that they wanted to send the message. A human at the other end would listen in another special way and know what the first one was thinking. Then if the message was not for them, they would turn and 'think' it along the next line until it got to where it had to go. The humans who did this wore long covers, the colour of snow, and would hold a bunch of mistletoe in their hands when they were 'thinking' the messages."

"Are you serious, or are you pulling our paws?" asked Tamarisk.

"Only passing on what my grandfather told me," Dandelion replied. "But the bit about following the lines is true, you saw it today. *I* can sense them and so can Spindle.

"The next thing my grandfather told me, even *I* find hard to believe. He may have been pulling *my* paw, he did sometimes." She smiled at the recollection. "He told me that at dawn, before the humans used the Leylines for messages, the squirrels did, in exactly the same way. Just face along the line the way you wanted to send a message and think. Of course there had to be a squirrel at the other end to receive it or it was a waste of time. I never knew whether to believe that.

"He also told me about Acorn, the first squirrel in the

world, and how he used to . . . But that's another story. I'll tell you that one tomorrow evening."

"Tell us now," demanded the squirrels, who loved a story.

Alder was about to check her but, on glancing at Marguerite, saw the tiny tail-flick indicating that a story might be good for morale. He nodded to Dandelion.

Chapter 31

"Once upon a time," Dandelion started, "there was Acorn, the first squirrel in the world.

"He sat in the First Great Oak, feeling lonely. All about him he could see other animals and birds and insects going about in pairs, mating and having youngsters or laying eggs and he thought, I'd like to have a mate like all these other creatures.

"So, that night he said a Needing Kernel to the Sun:

Oh Great Loving Sun
What I need most at this time –
Is another squirrel

but that didn't work because there were six sounds in the last line, not five – so he tried again:

Oh Great Loving Sun
What I need most at this time –
Is a Mate.

"But that only had three sounds, so he tried again:

Oh Great Loving Sun
What I need most at this time –
Is a loving Mate,

and the Sun, recognising the 5, 7, 5 sound pattern of a truly thought-out Kernel, arranged for Acorn to find a walnut in his drey when he woke up in the morning.

"Aha, he thought, the Sun is testing me; a walnut is not a mate, it's not even like a squirrel – but it's like a bird's egg. What's it like?" Dandelion looked at her audience seated round her in the dim burrow-light, listening intently.

"A bird's egg," they called back, enjoying the participation.

" 'Now what can I do with a bird's egg?' Acorn asked himself."

"Eat it?" called a voice from somewhere behind her and a laugh went through the audience.

"If he had done – none of us would be here now," Dandelion pointed out. She continued, "Maybe I can hatch it myself, Acorn thought, but then, as he sat outside his drey, he saw a woodcock come flying in through the trees below him to settle on its nest in the leaves on the ground.

"He climbed down and frightened the long-billed bird away. In the nest were three eggs which looked rather like walnuts, so Acorn carefully placed his special walnut egg in the nest, then climbed back up the tree and waited. Soon he saw the woodcock come jinking back through the trees to settle on the nest and brood, watching all about it with its eyes that are on the top of its head so that it can see in all directions at the same time.

"Every day after this, when the woodcock flew away to feed in the first swamp in the world, Acorn came down from his tree to listen at the nest. One day he heard the gentle tap, tap, tap of the woodcock chicks breaking out of their eggshells, so he carried his warm walnut up to his drey and sat there watching it. But nothing happened.

"He tried the What Do I Do Next Kernel:

Oh Great Loving Sun
You have set me a challenge
Help me to crack it,

and, as he said these words, he realised that all he had to do was to open *this* nut as he would any other.

"Carefully holding the precious brown nut, he split it open ever so gently and inside was – was – a tiny squirrel, all curled up and wet. He put down the empty halves of the shell and, holding the little red ball between his paws, he blew it dry, and as he did this it grew bigger and bigger, like a dragonfly does when it comes out of the water, until at last it was a perfect female squirrel.

"It was, of course, love at first sight. Acorn named her Primrose, which means the first of the flowers, as she *was* as pretty as a flower. Since then all true female squirrels are named after flowers, as all true male squirrels are named after trees.

"Acorn taught Primrose all he knew about foraging and drey-building and *she* taught him how to have fun and the joys of the mating chase. It was a very happy time for them both.

"Then one day, as they were playing in an oak tree,

Acorn picked an oak apple, young and brightly coloured green and red, and held it out to Primrose."

The squirrels nudged one another and giggled. They had all had that trick played on them, and in their turn had played it on others.

"Primrose took the beautiful thing and, trusting Acorn absolutely, bit into it.

"Not only was the oak apple bitter and nasty, but in the middle was a horrid little white grub, and to this day female squirrels never really trust males, *especially* when they bring gifts."

Dandelion looked round. The older females were nodding in agreement and the males were shaking their heads as if to say "That doesn't apply to me."

Marguerite slept little that night. As well as reviewing the first day's journey, she was wondering what the next day would have in store for them and was thinking through the implications of message-sending. How wonderful it would be if she could let her parents and her dear grandmother know that they were all alive and well.

At first light they set off northwards along the Leyline, heading for the Barrow of the Ferns, guided by Dandelion who stopped frequently to sense the direction of the force. They also needed regular rest periods as it was hard work dragging and pulling the Woodstock along. The older squirrels took turns to reconnoitre while the others rested, Juniper staying near to whichever pair of squirrels were in charge of the Woodstock, in case of a surprise attack by Greys.

As it happened, the precautions weren't needed. The country seemed empty of the enemy and each day's travel had been relatively uneventful. They had back-tracked on the refugees' route of the previous year, passing over the Barrow of the Ferns, the Water Barrow and the Drinking Barrow before turning almost due north towards the barrow where the three mysterious Lords had intercepted the fleeing party.

It was during one of the rest periods that Marguerite had another opportunity to talk to Dandelion about Earth forces.

The squirrels were, at this time, seated high in a tree looking out over the Army's tank and gunnery range, watching great brown and black patterned machines manoeuvring on the heath, distant and remote from them. They had seen the red flags marking the range boundaries but, as with so many of Man's structures and symbols, these meant nothing to the squirrels.

"What do *you* think makes the Greys' Stone force work?" Marguerite asked Dandelion.

These two females had come to respect each other's abilities in the time they had spent together and were now firm friends.

Dandelion looked around. The others were all out of ear-twitch. "They must tap one of Earth's hidden forces and focus it with the stone patterns. There are lots of forces we don't know much about. I know a little about the Leylines but my grandfather said that he believed that humans used an Earth force to find the north direction."

Marguerite looked puzzled. "Why would they need that? One only has to see where the moss on a tree grows to know which way is north, and on a clear night, if you poke your head out of your drey and look at the stars that make the Great Squirrel, you can see that its paws point to the star that is always in the north."

"Don't try and understand humans, my grandfather used to say. But they do know more about these things than we do. On our way south from Wolvesbarrow last year, we came to a line of huge metal trees that men must have made, with thin branches reaching from one to another. It was a wet day and some kind of force was blowing along those branches. We could hear it snapping and crackling and hissing and our whiskers were tingling and itching. We scampered under those, I can tell you."

Marguerite was silent, thinking of the force that made the Woodstock so powerful. Every squirrel knows the power of the Life-Force as it rises in the trees each spring. A sensitive squirrel can detect it moving upwards and outwards into every twig and leaf. She tried to picture the force rising in the hazel stem that formed the Woodstock *and* in the encircling honeysuckle bine, each trying to expand and outgrow the other. What a powerful but silent struggle this would be! The force would be trapped in the very fibres of the hazel, and held there in the form of a Woodstock, waiting to be released by *her* numbers.

A group of men were walking up the slope towards the tree, dressed in clothes the colour of ripe pine cones. The squirrels watched them through the leaves and saw them stop and stand in a group below where they sat. Occasionally one of the men would point across the heath and the others would hold black things up in front of their eyes.

Suddenly, from the straight branch projecting from one

of the machines in the distance, they saw a bright flash of light, followed by a loud crash. The squirrels ducked their heads instinctively. There was another flash and a crash from the hillside to their left and they ducked again.

"It looks as if humans have captured the thunder and lightning force," said Dandelion.

"I hope the Sun guides them to use it wisely," Marguerite replied. "It worries me sometimes, that if we tamper with forces we don't completely understand they may get out of control."

In all, two weeks on the march passed before they reached the Three Lords Barrow, which they approached warily.

There was no sign of the Lords, but they did find, under the furze bushes near the top of the mound, a squirrel skeleton with the remains of a grey tail attached.

"One less," said Alder, nosing at the remains disdainfully and, following the route pointed out by Dandelion, they turned south-west across a field and a roadway towards the Icen Barrow on the last-but-one leg to the Blue Pool.

Chapter 32

———

The squirrels crossed the roadway just before High Sun and passed through a small wood of chestnut and oak trees and were then on to heathland again.

"I can smell water. There must be a pool nearby," said Alder. "Although I can't remember seeing it on our way through here last year."

The scent was coming to them from somewhere south of the Leyline they were following, so the pool must be that way, hidden by the screen of pines on their right-paw side.

Tamarisk and Spindle, who were sent to find it, climbed one of the trees and looked down. The water was orangey brown and all around the edges were huge pink and white flowers set amongst dark green circular leaves. A heron was wading in the water near an Eyeland with three graceful trees on it.

If a heron was there, nothing dangerous was about. They slipped down the trunk and reported to the others.

"We'll break there," said Alder. "We could all use a rest and a drink."

Rowan was woken from sleep by a harsh squawk from his

187

guardian bird. The wary heron had just seen the party of strange squirrels appear on the top of the sand-cliff and, having vented his annoyance, had flown huffily away.

Something was about, thought Rowan, he must be careful, though he knew he was safer here on his Eyeland than on the mainland. He looked through a screen of twigs, then scratched himself to make sure he really was awake.

On the sand-cliff opposite stood his dear sister Marguerite, with Juniper, another squirrel without a tail whom he thought he had seen before, and "lots" of others; and, just behind them, he was sure he could see the face that had filled his dreams for a full year now. Could that really be Meadowsweet?

Now she had come to the edge of the sand-cliff and was looking towards the Eyeland.

"Meadowsweet," he called over the water, his voice breaking, "is it really you?"

"Rowan, my love!" she called back, oblivious of the stares of the other squirrels, and they all saw a squirrel leap from the upper branches of a tree on the Eyeland, to drop into the water and swim strongly ashore.

They all stood gaping as the wet animal scrabbled up the bank and hugged the slender female, their whiskers a-tangle. Then he turned to Marguerite who, realising who he was, had hopped nearer and was subjected to the same damp embrace.

"Rowan!"

"Meadowsweet, Marguerite! I thought I would never see either of you again."

"We thought you were caught by the fire . . ."

The excited squirrels chattered on, all talking at once,

until Alder interrupted, saying, "I greet you, Rowan, who I recall is tagged the Bold."

Rowan, remembering his manners, responded. "And I greet you . . . ?"

"Alder the Leader, father of Meadowsweet, whom you have soaked to the skin." He smiled at the handsome young squirrel as he said this, and Rowan grinned back.

". . . Alder the Leader, father of Meadowsweet, whom I have soaked to the skin and wish to have for my life-mate."

"You are well tagged, Rowan the Bold. If my Meadowsweet agrees, I would have no objection to such a mating."

The group foraged under the trees, drinking the sweet water and exchanging news. Rowan told how he had given up hope of finding the others alive after the fire and had crossed the Great Heath to this pool with his Eyeland, where he had learned to swim, so that he could live safely, surrounded by water, spending his time in celibacy and contemplation. Marguerite was intrigued to know that, despite all this time which he had been able to give to contemplation, he had not found out what came after eight, and she looked forward to explaining numbers to him later.

In their turn, they told him all that had happened to their parties in the past year, but how much Rowan took in, no squirrel could tell, for he did not take his eyes off Meadowsweet until the evening light faded.

They all climbed a tree near the shore of Rowan's Pool to sleep, having declined his offer to teach them to swim so that they could visit his magical Eyeland, but after it was dark, Marguerite was sure that she heard two soft splashes in the warm night. In the early dawn she saw Rowan and Meadowsweet licking each other dry on the shore below, but said nothing.

The party, now including Rowan, a little sorry to leave his Eyeland, moved off an hour later following the Leyline to the Icen Barrow where they disturbed a pair of deer lying up in a hollow under the vanilla-scented gorse that covered the mound. On the flattened grass in the sweetly smelling resting place of the deer, they held a Tagging Meeting, as Marguerite now felt able confidently to allocate meaningful tags to them all.

Dandelion was confirmed as the Ley Reader. Tamarisk's tag of the Tactless became the Forthright which he believed meant the same thing, but was pleased nevertheless. Spindle was tagged the Helpful because he always seemed to anticipate what other squirrels required and provided it, even before they realised their need themselves. Wood Anemone earned the tag of the Able because she could turn her paw to any task, no matter how great or small, and performed it without complaint. Both these squirrels were holding their tails high now.

Meadowsweet was tagged Rowan's Love as she seemed to have no life or interest beyond her love for him.

Juniper, to his great pleasure, was up-tagged the Steadfast.

Excitement was building when they left the Icen Barrow. They were nearing the Blue Pool area and although they did not expect to meet Greys in any numbers on the heathland, each knew that very soon they could be fighting against superior numbers of squirrels who would have the advantages of position, recent local knowledge, and, if they understood the term that Marble had once used to them, possession. Each was looking about nervously.

Dandelion reported with consternation that the Leyline from there to the great ruined Man-drey, which crossed the Blue Pool, was distorted and was behaving in an unusual way. "It's trying to curve away to the north and is breaking up," she told them. "Leylines don't do that. They are *always* perfectly straight. I don't know which way to go. We could miss your pool altogether."

The heat-haze over the heath hid any distant landmarks, even clumps of trees nearby were shimmering and insubstantial, so Alder called a halt and the senior squirrels got together to reformulate plans.

"We don't want to take on the Greys in unfamiliar countryside," Alder stated. "We must be in an area we know if we are going to surprise them. Remember, there are lots more of them than there are of us."

"Even more than when we left, they will have had a whole breeding year since then," Juniper added.

"*I* know this area," said Rowan. "I came through here on my way back from climbabout. At the end of the heath is a field, then a roadway, then a field shaped like a dog's leg, then it's the edge of the Beachend Guardianship. We need to go *this* way."

"Now for the Greys," said Juniper.

"Right," said Tamarisk.

Rowan was correct. That evening they reached the roadway, crossed the Dogleg Field and gathered together in the corner of the wood at the extreme western tip of the old Beachend Guardianship, whispering excitedly and watching for any sign of Greys.

"We should wait until morning before we go in," Marguerite advised Alder. "When we hear the big gates open it will be safer, as the Greys are less likely to attack us if Visitors are about."

Alder acknowledged her local experience and ordered a withdrawal back across the Dogleg Field to spend a watchful night in a hedgerow tree.

"My whiskers ache," Marguerite heard Tamarisk say in the morning.

"So do mine," said Dandelion, "I thought it was from the strain of following the Leylines."

The squirrels reported that they all had an unusual dull ache around the base of their whiskers, but none could suggest an explanation.

The sun was hidden by an early mist as they started off again, Marguerite hopping eagerly in front. Near the corner of the wood Alder called to her and she stopped. He told the others to position themselves some yards out in the field.

"You stay here in charge, Juniper," Alder instructed him. "When we hear that gate, I'll go with Marguerite to discover where the Greys are. Keep the Woodstock here. If you see any Greys, use it. *Don't* take any chances. You're responsible for the safety of this group. Keep the others behind you, mount the Woodstock on this mound – that way you can cover all the ground from here to the wood-edge – but *don't* power it at us by mistake when we come back!"

Having ensured that the Woodstock was on firm, raised ground, they waited for the sound of the gate, then, her heart thumping with excitement, Marguerite led Alder into the familiar woodland surrounding the Blue Pool.

Chapter 33

The mist had thinned out and drifted away and the sun was shining above them as the pair entered the trees, the shadows in the wood seeming unusually deep and sharp. Marguerite scented the air. This was her home! That was the water-scent, this was the home-pine smell, different in some subtle way from that of pines in all the other places through which she had travelled.

All around was the leaf-litter smell and on the paths the scents left by the Visitors from the day before stirred memories of happier days.

They climbed a tree, and then she and Alder moved cautiously through the Beachend treetops towards Humanside, watchful for any grey shapes in the trees, in the bushes, or on the ground below. None was to be seen and there did not even seem to be any scent of Greys. Nevertheless she led the way cautiously, startled at one point by a noisy rustling of leaves from the ground, but it was only a male blackbird searching for food. At last, they looked down on to the pool she loved.

It was no longer blue!

There seemed to be tiny vibrations disturbing the water,

hardly noticeable in themselves, yet enough to spoil any reflections, even on a day as bright as this one. The Blue Pool was just a dull grey colour.

Marguerite and Alder circled past the Man-dreys, seeing the Red-Haired Girl and the Human Who Picked Things Up talking on the steps, but with no sign of any scavenging Greys around the tables. Then on through Deepend to Steepbank where together they climbed up the old Council Tree. There were strange dreys there, but most were in a state of disrepair.

"I think the Greys have left," Marguerite whispered to Alder.

"Do you really?" he asked, hopefully.

"The Sun has been good to us. But . . ." She looked up through the pine needles, then down at the water. It should have been blue but it still wasn't. Something was seriously wrong. And her whiskers were aching intolerably.

Juniper was restless as he crouched behind the Woodstock waiting for hordes of savage Greys to come charging out of the wood to overwhelm him. Hot as it was, he struggled to stay alert, ready to defend his charges, should the enemy appear. As long as the Woodstock worked as well on the Greys as it had on The Nipper, they should be all right, he thought. The rest of the party dozed in the sun-warm grass behind him.

His eyelids kept closing in the drowsy heat and he forced himself to stay awake. *He* had been left in charge. He imagined Marguerite's contempt if she found him asleep at his post. What terrible tag would she give him then: Juniper the Dozy, or Juniper Who Risked the Lives of his

Friends by Sleeping? He stretched and walked around in a circle. "Sun, it's hot!" A movement at the wood-edge caught his eye and he scurried back to position himself behind the Woodstock.

As he watched, a grey squirrel hopped out from under the trees and scented the air. Juniper rotated the weapon so that it was aimed directly at the Grey and then reached forward to scratch a number as he had done a houndread times in practice on the Tout. His elbow locked. He could not move it forward. This was another *squirrel* he was about to kill in cold blood! That would make him no better than the Greys who had killed Bluebell at the poolside. He remembered Alder's instructions and went to reach forward again. Marguerite would be livid if she knew he had disobeyed the Leader's clear orders. She might even be watching, but still he could not bring himself to scratch the number on the grey twist of the Woodstock after the X.

The Grey hopped nearer, watching Juniper on the mound. He paused, stood to his full height and called out, keeping his tail low, "I come as a friend."

Juniper looked at him for a moment, then said, "Come forward slowly – very slowly. I only have to touch *this* and you're Sun-gone for sure. Are there more of you in the wood?"

"No. There is only me left now. All the other Silvers are gone. Grey Death has taken them. Every last one, but me," he added sadly, spreading his forelimbs as he said it.

Juniper saw then that the Grey had a paw missing.

The other squirrels had woken on hearing the voices and were gathering in a group behind Juniper and the Woodstock.

"A Grey, a Grey," shouted Tamarisk. "Get him with the Woodstock, Juniper, get him."

"No. Stay where you are and watch the wood-edge, I don't know if we can trust him. It may be a trick."

When Alder and Marguerite returned, soon after High Sun, to report the mysterious absence of any other squirrels, they were amazed to find the party grouped around a single Grey, with the Woodstock lying discarded on the mound. Marguerite looked sharply at Juniper, then at the Grey.

She recognised him. "Marble?" she asked.

"Yes, Bright Marguerite, it's me, Marble. Known to most as Three Paws," he added wryly. "The one who taught you the meaning of power when we first met. You were a dreyling then."

"Where are the other Greys?" she asked coldly.

"I was telling your friends how all the silver squirrels but me caught the Grey Death. Only your Sun knows how I avoided it. Even the biggest Power Square ever built couldn't protect them."

Chapter 34

Sure now that Marble was alone, they had all moved out of the heat into the cool of the wood and gathered round to hear his story. Marguerite had quietly told Juniper to stay at the back of the group with the Woodstock near him, "just in case".

Marble began. "At first, there were only a few sick squirrels. A new batch of colonists had just arrived from Woburn, travelling fast, and they had only taken about two moons to come all the way. They were what we call a 'randee' lot. No respect for the old moral standards, just mated with any squirrel they fancied at the time. But that's beside the point.

"They were allocated territories in New New England – you used to call that precinct Steepbank – and settled in well, but they would often go over to New Connecticut and mingle with the Silvers there. You remember Gabbro? He used to tell me what was going on. Such parties! As I said, they were a randee lot.

"Then a week or so later some of the local Silvers took poorly, nothing you could put your claw on, so to speak, they just looked a mite peaky and then within a few days they were, what do you so quaintly call it, Sun-gone?"

"What do you call it?" Marguerite asked.

"Zapped," replied Marble. "But call it what you like, they were gone. My friend Gabbro was one of the first to go. He loved those Randees.

"Then it started happening all over. There were squirrels falling out of trees like chestnuts in a gale. None ever recovered. The odd thing about it was that the Grey Death did not seem to get the very elderly, or the dreylings until they reached mating age. The old ones and the youngsters are usually the first to catch any sickness that's about. This seemed different. We called it 'Grey Death' because it made the silver fade out of our fur and just leave it dull. I went over to New Connecticut to help out but there was nothing much I could do.

"Then the Three Lords came through and gave orders that a giant Power Square was to be built on the dried-out Clay-Pan. They said it would protect us from the Grey Death. All Silvers, sick or well, were to collect and lay out stones. *Each side* was to have this many."

(Here Marble made this symbol with a stick and six fir cones.

"It took three weeks just to collect them. Many squirrels were so ill that they didn't survive this work, and collapsed and died while searching and carrying. I seemed to be the fittest, but with a paw missing I couldn't carry, so I was laying out the stones line after line after line. Sun, was I tired!"

*64 rows of 64 = 4096 total.

He paused to judge the effect his story was having on the Reds. They were spellbound. Feeling some of his old pleasure when holding an audience, he continued, "I had to leave out certain key and corner stones or I would have been overcome by the Power myself. A block of four larger keystones in the very centre, and the four corner stones, had to be added last. That was dangerous work. Finally I rolled in the keystones, positioned those and then had to run for my life down between two of the rows as the Power started to build up.

"At the same time four other squirrels had been selected to place the corner stones. The Lords had not told them that it was to be *their* body-power that would be used to start the force and not one of the four got clear."

"But you did, obviously," said Tamarisk.

"Yes, I was fit even if I was tired. I got away over the bank just in time. The Three Lords didn't. They wanted to stay and see it work. They were so proud of what they had had us make that they just sat on the top of the bank staring down. I watched them fall one by one. Then I ran away." He paused.

"So no Greys survived but you?" Alder asked.

"I am the only Silver left now," replied Marble, "so it was all to no avail and the Power Square will run for ever."

"Was it the square-thing that saved you?" asked Tamarisk.

"No. Grey Death has just passed me by, I think," Marble replied.

"Is it the Power Square that makes everything feel odd round here?" asked Juniper. "My whiskers have been aching all day."

"Mine too," said Dandelion. "And it was probably the Power Square affecting the Leyline and the colour of the pool."

"We must destroy it," said Marguerite.

"Impossible," said Marble.

"Nothing is impossible," responded Marguerite and her voice continued:

> *If you think you can*
> *Or if you think you cannot,*
> *Either way it's true.*

"Tomorrow we destroy that square," said Alder decisively.

"We must ask the Sun for help," said Dandelion unexpectedly.

"We will," replied Marguerite. "But also remember one of Old Burdock's favourite Kernels."

> *Your prayers alone*
> *Will not do. The Sun will help*
> *Those who help themselves.*

The lone Grey joined them as they prayed, closing his eyes and keeping his tail low.

Chapter 35

Marble had shown a marked reluctance to leave them as darkness fell. They were still discussing ways of destroying the Power Square until finally Alder told him that they were retreating for the night and if he was going to help, he could meet them here at the wood-edge just after dawn. With some hesitation, Marble left them and the Reds recrossed the Dogleg Field, taking the Woodstock with them.

Marguerite and Dandelion were together, talking, as Juniper and Tamarisk dragged it along through the grass behind them.

"Do you really think that all the Greys are dead?" Dandelion asked.

"You sound like Chestnut, who used to be one of the Guardians of Deepend," Marguerite said. "He was tagged the Doubter. But yes, I think Marble is telling the truth. Did you notice that he joined our prayers? It's strange to have come all this way fearing the Greys, only to find a different enemy."

Tamarisk, who had overheard the conversation, tapped the Woodstock and said optimistically, "With this we can zap Greys or stones."

"I don't know if zap is the right word for stones," Marguerite said, "but with the help of the Sun, tomorrow we'll find out."

Marble was waiting, as agreed, at the edge of the wood and he foraged with the Reds, his tail conspicuously low, and again joined in their prayers, before they all moved off towards the Clay-Pan, the aches in their whisker-roots growing more painful with every tree they passed. They went through woodland and patches of scrub familiar to Marguerite, Juniper, Rowan and Tamarisk, until they came to the edge of the area they had last seen devastated by the fire in the previous year. In place of the blackened, smoking mass of ash and charred heather stems, a forest of the tall, feathery stems of rosebay-willowherb waved in the breeze, releasing their fluffy seeds to drift away and colonise any other newly exposed ground before the native plants could re-establish themselves.

The squirrels moved through the stems, noting the new bright green shoots sprouting from the bases of the heather plants and the mosses and lichens beginning to cover the burnt-over ground.

As they neared the Clay-Pan and their whisker-aches grew almost unbearable, they saw how even the rosebay plants were stunted and the heather shoots weaker. The rim of the hollow containing the Clay-Pan was barren of vegetation of any kind.

They flattened themselves to the ground, wriggled to the edge and peered over. Just as Marble had described it, the clay surface was covered with line after line of stones, each one in perfect alignment, and in the very centre of the square were the four keystones, larger than the rest. Next to each corner stone lay the dried-up body of a grey squirrel.

Waves of sickening Power washed over the Reds and they moved back to crouch in the stunted growth, out of sight of the square.

"Look," said Marguerite, "all the needles on that tree are withered up."

She was pointing to the old fir in which they had hidden from the Grey posse the previous summer. It still leaned out over the Clay-Pan and had been exposed to the Power of the square ever since it had been activated by the deaths of the four Greys.

"Any ideas?" she asked the nervous squirrels.

"There might be one way," said Marble. "If I were to run out along that tree trunk and drop on to the keystones, I should be able to disrupt the Power for long enough for four of you to displace the corner stones."

"It'll kill you," said Marguerite, "and the other four."

"Probably the first and possibly the second," replied Marble. "Have you got any better ideas?"

"We should try the Woodstock," said Juniper.

The Woodstock was brought up and sighted first on to the keystones and then on to each corner stone in turn. Juniper tried first but, having scratched every number from 2 as far as 7 after the X, there was no noticeable effect. The spiralling power surged from the Woodstock as before, but was deflected upwards and lost in the withered needles of the overhanging fir.

He tried again and again and then had to retire, vomiting from the effects of the Stone force that he had been exposed to.

Marguerite tried but was no more successful, then Rowan, who, though unfamiliar with the weapon, insisted on trying until he too was forced back from the rim of the Clay-Pan.

Tamarisk tried, but he soon reported that the force from the Woodstock must be exhausted as he could get no response, whatever number he scratched.

"Are you really prepared to drop on to the keystones?" Alder asked Marble. "You'll be Sun-gone in an instant."

"I'll kick those stones out of line first," he replied. "I owe you this for the trouble we Silvers have brought you." There was a look of grim determination in his eyes.

Alder looked at him, then around the group and said, "Now I want three volunteers to help me deal with the corner stones."

"I'll be one," said Juniper the Steadfast and was immediately joined by Tamarisk the Forthright and Rowan the Bold. Meadowsweet put a restraining paw on Rowan's shoulder but he turned, brushed whiskers with her and moved over to where Alder was giving instructions.

"Act only when Marble has dropped, then we'll rush out of cover and kick away the corner stones. Don't miss. Trust in the Sun."

They moved off to get into position.

"The Sun be with you," Marguerite called to Marble and he acknowledged this by putting the stump of his paw diagonally across his chest, then crouched and wriggled to the base of the tree trunk. Here he paused, feeling the vibrations with his three good paws as the Power broke down the very fibres within the tree. He raised his head and watched the red volunteers get into their places.

"Now," he shouted, "now, now!" and ran awkwardly on his three paws, up and along the sloping trunk before launching himself through the air, to land, kicking and scrabbling amongst the stones below.

There was no change in the Power waves. He had missed the keystones!

Alder, crouched as near as he could to the corner stone he was to displace, watched in horror as Marble's kicking slowed to a spasmodic twitch. He ran forward, signalling to the other volunteers to do the same, but was repelled by the Stone force and rolled back, covered in dry clay-dust.

The other squirrels were having no more success. "Again," he called, "again." It was like leaping upwind in a gale.

After three more attempts, he signalled "retreat"; they crawled back to join the others sheltering beyond the bank and the volunteers lay in the dust retching and vomiting, hardly able to move.

"Is Marble Sun-gone?" Alder asked.

"Yes," said Marguerite. "A brave squirrel, despite his colour."

When they had recovered somewhat they sat in a circle, each trying to think of some new way to destroy the evil thing on the Clay-Pan. It was Tamarisk who spoke out at last.

"There's nothing else for it. One of *us* is going to have to scatter the keystones."

Rowan, without thinking further, started towards the leaning tree, saw Meadowsweet out of the corner of his eye, turned to give her a farewell hug and as he did so collided with Alder who was heading for the tree himself. Both squirrels, disoriented by the effect of their ordeal in the Clay-Pan, fell over and rolled in the dust which rose in clouds and blinded them.

Marguerite had been looking at the fir tree as Tamarisk was speaking, seeing its brown and sickly foliage, and thinking of the Power spreading out to destroy other beautiful trees. Would her pool ever be blue again? She stood up and moved deliberately towards the leaning fir trunk.

Juniper, who as usual was watching her, realised her intention and, sick as he was, gathered his strength, ran towards the tree, shouldered her roughly out of the way and leapt for the leaning trunk.

He scrabbled to hold on, a piece of rotten bark turning to powder under his claws as he dug deeper, searching for firm wood. It was as though the whole tree was punkwood and would give him no grip. Marguerite was on the trunk behind him. Juniper tried to kick her away.

Then, as though the tiny additional weight of the squirrels was too much, the ancient tree, rotten through from the continuous Power waves, with no sound other than the rustling of the dead and dying needles, collapsed and fell on to the clay.

Juniper and Marguerite jumped clear as the trunk shattered on the hard-baked ground, brittle branches breaking off and, in falling, sweeping away and destroying the pattern and the Power of the stones for ever.

The force died with a whimper, more felt than heard, and in the silence that followed a skylark sang high over the Great Heath.

Marguerite stood up, and embraced Juniper silently. "Now to the pool," she said, dusting the clay-dust from her fur. "Faith *can* fell fir trees."

Later, on the sweet-scented pine needles below the Council Tree at Steepbank, she spoke to the squirrels at a special meeting called by Alder, the pool a bright sapphire blue below them.

"We all have a job to do. We must repopulate this lovely land. Each pair of you can choose a Guardianship. Go now, there is some serious mating to be done."

She turned her rump to Juniper the Steadfast, who, scenting her readiness, needed no second bidding as she raced away through the treetops, closely pursued by him.

1, 2, 3 . . .

Chapter 36

On Ourland, Fern had wanted Oak to take over Ex-King
Willow's drey in the magnificent Royal Macrocarpa Tree
behind Brownsea Castle. Oak had refused, even though
Ex-King Willow and Ex-Kingz Mate Thizle had moved
out themselves to a more humble drey near the lagoon.

"It wouldn't be right, my dear," he explained. "All that
kind of thing is past. We've quietly got to change things to
a more sensible arrangement. But we *do* need a new drey
in a more central position. Let's go and find a site near the
pond in Beech Valley."

The Royal Macrocarpa itself, now abandoned by the
squirrels, possibly just being over-mature, or perhaps
sensing the shame of the injustice witnessed in its
branches, was in decline and losing its foliage in showers
with every breeze. By the Longest Day it was a bare
skeleton of a tree.

Oak and Old Burdock were together in the new Council
Tree near the Beech Valley pond. The tree was a full-
grown beech, rooted on the very edge of the pool which,
though smaller by far than the Blue Pool, still sent up a

delicious water-scent on hot days. The clicking and whirring of dragonflies' wings below reminded them of home.

The water-lilies in the pond they had recognised as being the kind of flowers that Rowan had described as being at the Eyeland pool he had found while on climbabout, in those peaceful days before the Greys had come to spoil it all.

Burdock was a very old squirrel now.

"You have so many grey hairs I thought it was Marble come again," Oak had "pulled her paw", as she hauled herself breathlessly up the trunk to stretch out on the wide branch, shaded from the sun by the canopy of glossy green leaves.

"We must appoint a new Tagger," she told him, looking down at the water and the lilies, "I'll be Sun-gone soon."

"We'll all miss you," Oak told her warmly. "I can't imagine not having you about, with a Kernel for every occasion."

"My time is near and I'm ready for when the Sun calls me. To be honest I'm so tired nowadays I'm quite looking forward to the rest. It's nice to know that my old body will be feeding the trees that I have fed from for so long. It makes a sort of circle. A kind of fair deal."

She spoke slowly now and when a Kernel was needed, it seemed to come from way, way down in her mind.

"I must train a successor," she said, after a long pause. "I had been hoping that Marguerite would come back. She was a natural Tagger, but Sun knows where she is now." She paused again, looking round wistfully as though expecting to see the Bright One appear.

"Clover the Carer is my next choice; one learns a lot about squirrel-nature looking after the sick ones."

"Is there a lot to teach her?" Oak asked.

"Well, she knows all the Basic Kernels, but the skill is in recalling the right one at the right time, and saying it with just the degree of confidence for the others to be strengthened or guided by it. I think I've nearly got it right myself at last," she added with a modesty that made Oak, himself an elderly squirrel now, smile affectionately. "But I do wish I knew if Marguerite was all right."

"She will be," Oak assured her. "She's a survivor, that one. And she's got that old reprobate, Juniper, looking after her. She'll be fine. Probably made me a grandfather by now, if I but knew it." Oak, in his turn, looked wistful.

Oak was right. Marguerite, more to her own surprise than that of her companions, had accepted Juniper as her life-mate and they had destroyed the abandoned dreys in the Deepend Guardianship and together had built a new one where they could look out over the Blue Pool.

Juniper had a favourite lying-out place from which he could see the beach where Bluebell had died from her injuries the previous summer. Marguerite was wise enough not to resent this, and was pleased that he never ventured near the Man-dreys and the temptation of the salted nuts, though she could sense that even now he sometimes craved them.

She, in her turn, had a favourite lying-out place at the eastern side of the Guardianship, in a high Look-out Pine where she could see over Middlebere Heath to Poole Harbour and Ourland. She would lie in the branches for hours thinking of ways to send messages to her family there.

There *must* be a way. Dolphins could send messages into her mind through the air as well as through the water, she was sure that the great ship that passed them at sea had been sending messages and Dandelion had told how, long ago, men had sent messages along the Leylines. Even squirrels, if she could believe the legend, had once used the Leylines at dawn in a similar way.

She had asked Dandelion to sense for a Leyline which might lead from the Blue Pool to Ourland for there were dreylings stirring inside her and she wanted to tell her family.

Dandelion, herself heavy with young, was unable to find such a line, sitting in the Look-out Pine and turning her head slowly from side to side, sensing with the utmost concentration, aware of the intensity of Marguerite's desire.

"Trust in the Sun," she reminded her friend. "Faith can fell fir trees," she added, putting a comforting paw on Marguerite's shoulder. "We know *that* is true."

Marguerite gave life to two new squirrels a week later, one male and one female. Juniper had waited all night in the warm summer darkness outside the drey. Now as the sun rose, she called him in. "Names first," she said. "Tags when they're older."

In the dim light of the drey they looked at the bald pink creatures squirming blindly on the soft mossy lining, and saw handsome youngsters running and leaping with joy in the sunshine.

Juniper looked at the tiny female, opened his mouth to

suggest Bluebell, thought better of it and said, "Oak and Burdock?"

"That would be my choice too," said Marguerite.

On the same day Rowan came proudly and breathlessly over from Humanside to tell Juniper and Marguerite that his Meadowsweet had borne a female dreyling and that they would like to call her Bluebell to honour the squirrel who had given her life to save the whole colony from the Greys; and would Juniper mind?

Juniper looked as proud as he had earlier, when he had looked on his own first-born.

Soon afterwards, news came from Steepbank that Alder and Dandelion were also parents again, and the next day Spindle the Helpful came to see if he was needed for anything and after a while, casually told them that Wood Anemone had also borne twins on the previous day.

Tamarisk, unmated that year, raced around the pool visiting each drey as proudly as if he had been responsible for all the new lives. It was remembered as a High-Tail Time for them all.

Chapter 37

Marguerite's duties as a parent and as the Tagger kept her mind off the desire to contact the Ourlanders for a whole moon, but then the urge to communicate came back with even greater force than before. Her mind constantly reviewed everything she could recall about signals, messages and forces. She awoke one night with a picture of the Woodstock before her and at first light she slipped away to the Clay-Pan to find it.

She found the weapon, near to where they had discarded it, half sunk in a puddle of slimy clay from overnight rain, and dragged it out to dry. The sky was still heavily overcast but a light breeze eventually turned the slime on the wood to a smooth white covering through which her numbers were still visible, but as she had feared, there was now no power in it. Try as she would with any combination of figures following her X, no force of any kind was left. It *was* all expended when we used it against the square, she thought, and, abandoning the exhausted Woodstock amongst the scattered stones and the crushed branches of the fallen fir, she set out to return to Deepend through the hazel copse.

The green-fringed nuts were filling but were not yet ready to harvest, and, as she assessed the likely crop, the sun broke through the clouds as it had done for her once before, a single ray of sunshine again lighting for a moment the hazel sapling being strangled by the honeysuckle bine.

A new Woodstock! The message was clear. With her strong white teeth she cut through the bitter-tasting stem of the woodbine and then into the hazel bark, tasting tantalisingly of the developing nuts themselves.

When the distorted, tortured stem had been dragged to the ground, she trimmed it to the same length as the first Woodstock, feeling, as she did so, the power-tingle in her whiskers that she had always felt when handling that one.

Marguerite looked up through the leaves at the sun, now shining brightly from a clearing sky.

"Thank you," she said quietly, "thank you."

High in the Council Tree in Beech Valley the United Ourlanders were gathered for that day's study of Kernels, Traditions and Manners. Old Burdock was speaking slowly, "Every squirrel should know . . ."

She stopped, as though listening to leaf-whispers from far, far away, then in quite a different voice said, "Marguerite is talking to me . . . Marguerite is talking to me . . . She . . . and Juniper are life-mated and have borne two dreylings . . . they have named them . . . Oak and . . . and . . . Burdock . . ." (Her old face lit up.) ". . . Rowan is alive . . . as Bold as ever . . . he has life-mated with Meadowsweet . . . they have a dreyling named . . . named . . . Bluebell . . . Spindle and Wood Anemone . . . Zpider and Woodlouze . . . have borne twins . . . There are no

Greys at the Blue Pool . . . Tamarisk is on climba . . ."

Old Burdock's voice was failing, she was using every last remnant of her strength to catch the whisper in the air. Then as it faded, she turned towards the tiny clump of trees on the far-away skyline, focused her entire body-energy into one concentrated thought, magnified by the love she and all those around her felt, and sent it leaping out of her body and across the water to the distant heathlands.

"We have heard you, Marguerite. We *have* heard you."

Her body slumped exhausted on the broad grey-green branch of the beech tree and Clover moved forward to sit by her, a paw on the frail shoulder of her teacher and friend. She could feel the slowing of Old Burdock's breathing. All was silence except for a gentle breeze rustling the beech leaves about them.

At last Old Burdock raised her eyes to the sky, blinked at the bright light and said:

> *Sun, now let me come,*
> *Peacefully, to you. Your gift*
> *To a true Tagger.*

Clover reached forward and closed the lids of Old Burdock's vacant eyes. Fern combed out the last few hairs of her tail.

> *Sun, take this squirrel*
> *Into the peace of your earth*
> *To nourish a tree.*

Away over the water and the heath, Marguerite took her

paw from the New Woodstock and leant back exhausted against the trunk of the Look-out Pine.

"I reached them," she whispered to Juniper, "I reached them. The Key is 12345670 × *42*."

No wonder they called her the Bright One, Juniper thought lovingly, as he helped her back to the drey above the pool of sapphire blue where young Oak and Burdock were sleeping the sleep of the innocent.

Epilogue

Should you be in Dorset, in the south of England, known to some as New America, and take a boat out to Brownsea Island you will, if you are lucky, and quiet, see some of the descendants of the United Ourlanders.

The New Council Tree is there in Beech Valley but the "Tree that Died of Shame" is now only a grey stump and you will find this a few yards south of the church, often with a royal-looking peacock perched on it. The human Guardians of the Island, The National Trust, have planted another tree nearby.

You can visit Pottery Point and see the broken pipes and chimney pots from the vanished pottery where the exiles came ashore on the old door so long ago, and where Next-King Sallow met his just deserts. Around the corner past the pier you may find the steps down through the pine trees and rhododendron bushes to Woodstock Bay.

The boy who lost his rubber dinghy in a whirlwind must be grown up now and, should he read this, will at last know what happened to it and how it became the new Sun's-child and saved Marguerite's tail.

You can, when the Army decree, visit the abandoned

Man-dreys of Tyneham and climb Worbarrow Tout and the Barrow of the Flowers, where, even without whiskers, you might just be able to sense the ancient Leylines leading away over the land to Wolvesbarrow and beyond.

You will *not* find red squirrels at the beautiful Blue Pool. This is once again inhabited by Greys, still insisting that they be called Silvers, but they are altogether a gentler breed than the harsh and randee adventurers of the old pioneering days of Marble, his friend Gabbro and their long Sun-gone compatriots.

In the Museum at the Blue Pool is the original Woodstock from Brownsea Island, found many years later in the Clay-Pan and now preserved there for the benefit of non-believers.

What became of Bright Marguerite, Juniper the Steadfast, Tamarisk the Forthright, Rowan the Bold, Meadowsweet and all the other Reds who had adventured together? That, as Dandelion, the Ley Reader, would have said, is another story.

Michael Tod
Llangattock
January 1993

Notes

WOODSTOCKS

THE WOODSTOCKS of the story are not as rare as one might expect, and may be found anywhere that honeysuckle thrives.

Wild honeysuckle (*Lonicera periclymenun*), or woodbine as it is sometimes called, grows in woodland and along hedgerows. It tries to find a host plant, usually a young tree or a sapling, to climb up, always twisting in a clockwise direction, until, when it can climb no further, it will bush out and produce sweetly scented, trumpet-shaped flowers.

Woodstocks are formed when the honeysuckle stem is wound so tightly round the stems of the other plant that it constricts growth. Often the bine is loosely wound and this allows the other stem to expand normally but, when it cannot do so, it will grow into the barley-sugar-shaped Woodstock. If the host can grow faster than the honeysuckle, it may break the bine or form a spiral burr covering sections of it entirely. Conversely, if the honeysuckle grows faster, it will often kill the host through strangulation.

The months of December to March are the best times to

find a Woodstock. As honeysuckle grows mostly in the shade of other plants, it has adapted to steal a march on the others by coming into leaf early, often before the old year is dead. At this time they are virtually the only new leaves to be seen in a winter woodland and they light up like green candle flames if the sun is shining.

I always get a thrill out of seeing the green mass amongst the stark winter branches and searching up each host stem to see if a Woodstock has formed there.

The best ones seem to be on hazel, but I have found them on ash, willow, beech and once even on a Norway spruce (the Christmas tree) where the Woodstock had formed about fifteen feet up. Honeysuckle often grows up hawthorn bushes but I have not yet found a Woodstock on one of these.

I believe that sheep may eat young honeysuckle shoots, so if sheep have regular access to the area, you are unlikely to find any honeysuckle at all, let alone a Woodstock.

I collected a number of Woodstocks while researching this book, and Phil Drabble has a walking stick made from one (you can see it in the photograph on the front of one of his books), but I would urge you to leave any that *you* find growing for others to discover and appreciate. If all the people that I hope will read this book go searching them out and collecting them, there would soon be none left in the wild.

THE BLUE POOL

THE BLUE POOL at Furzebrook, between Wareham and Corfe Castle on Dorset's Isle of Purbeck, has attracted and enchanted visitors for over fifty years. Purbeck clay has been mined in this area for centuries, and the Blue Pool was excavated for this purpose in the mid-1880s. Its fame as a beauty spot originally came from the curious fact that the hue of the water changes from minute to minute with every variation of sunshine, cloud and rain. At one moment it might be a shade of green or blue, and in the next turn to rich turquoise, and this phenomenon still holds a unique fascination.

The pool is the centrepiece of the Furzebrook estate, surrounded by twenty-five acres of heathland comprising heather and gorse, pine and silver birch. There are many indigenous species of plants and animals to be seen, some so rare that the estate has been designated a Site of Special Scientific Interest.

However, no study of the natural delights of the Blue Pool and its environment will uncover the complex social history that links the very existence of the pool with such diverse characters and events as Sir Walter Raleigh and the tobacco trade, the seventeenth-century fashion for periwigs, the China tea trade and Josiah Wedgwood. To do this it is necessary to visit the Blue Pool Museum.

The grounds are open from March to November. The Tea House, Gift Shop, Museum, Plant Centre are open from Easter to October. (Signposted at the southern end of the Wareham by-pass.)

The Blue Pool, Furzebrook, Wareham, Dorset. Telephone: 0929 551408.

BROWNSEA ISLAND

BROWNSEA ISLAND is owned and cared for by The National Trust, the UK's most active independent conservation charity, and is a peaceful haven set in the middle of bustling Poole Harbour.

A beautiful 500-acre island of heath and woodland, Brownsea features miles of woodland walks and open glades and magnificent views of the Dorset coast.

Home to a huge variety of wildlife, including peacocks, terns, waders and wildfowl, it is one of the few places where the red squirrel survives in England.

There is also a 200-acre nature reserve, managed by the Dorset Trust for Nature Conservation, with access for guided parties at fixed times.

Brownsea Island is open from April to September, daily from 10 a.m. until 8 p.m. (or dusk if earlier). Passenger ferries depart every thirty minutes from Poole Quay or Sandbanks.

For more information write to Head Warden, Brownsea Island, Poole Harbour, BH15 1EC. Telephone: 0202 707744.

RED AND GREY SQUIRRELS
IN BRITAIN

The native red squirrels (*Sciurus vulgaris*) were once common over much of Great Britain and Ireland and were so plentiful in places that they were treated as vermin and shot on sight.

They prefer coniferous woodland but can thrive in deciduous woods and eat a wide variety of foods including nuts and catkins, tree buds, fungi, berries, pine seeds and insects.

Grey squirrels (*Sciurus carolinensis*) are natives of the east coast of North America and were introduced to the British Isles in the late 1800s at several places, the best known of which was Woburn Park. From these locations they have spread out to cover most of England and Wales and parts of Scotland. They were also introduced into Ireland.

Greys are more at home in deciduous woodland, but their diet is very similar to that of the Reds, and since they are more ready to accept urban environments than Reds, they have also adapted to eat much "foreign food" from bird tables.

I have to admit that, although only the Greys in the story are shown as killing young birds, both Reds and Greys have been recorded as doing so. Both bury excess food in the autumn and find it again, by scent, in the winter. They do not remember where each cache is, but rely on their noses to find the food they or another squirrel buried.

Contrary to popular belief squirrels do not hibernate in the winter, although they do become much less active than in summer and prefer to stay in their dreys when it is very cold, wet or windy.

Unlike those of the Blue Pool Demesne, squirrels do not normally mate for life and male squirrels play no part in bringing up their offspring. They can produce two litters per year, each litter averaging three youngsters. However, mortality is high and about eighty per cent don't make their first birthday. Five is a good old age for a squirrel.

It is easy to mistake a grey squirrel for a red in poor light as Greys do have a lot of brown hairs, but they are generally bigger and more heavily built than the Reds. They do not interbreed.

"Grades" is not an actual ailment of squirrels but they do suffer from epidemic diseases including Coccidiosis and Parapoxvirus.

Should you want to make a further study of these engaging animals I can recommend *Squirrels* by Jessica Holm, published by Whittet Books.